GARY CHUDLEIGH . TANYA ROBERTS

PLAGUED

THE MIRANDA CHRONICLES

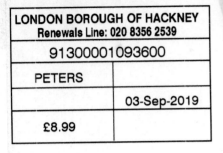

Written by: **Gary Chudleigh**

Art by: **Tanya Roberts**

Letters by: **Colin Bell**

Flats by: **Ludwig Olimba**

Edited by: **Jack Lothian and Sha Nazir**

Publication design by: **Kirsty Hunter**

Front and Back Cover illustration by: **Tanya Roberts**

Cover Design by: **Sha Nazir**

First printing 2018

Published in Glasgow by BHP Comics Ltd

ISBN: 978-1-910775-19-6

Made in Scotland. Printed in Great Britain by
Bell & Bain Ltd, Glasgow

A CIP catalogue reference for this book is available from the
British Library

Ask your local comic or bookshop to stock BHP Comics

Visit www.BHPComics.com

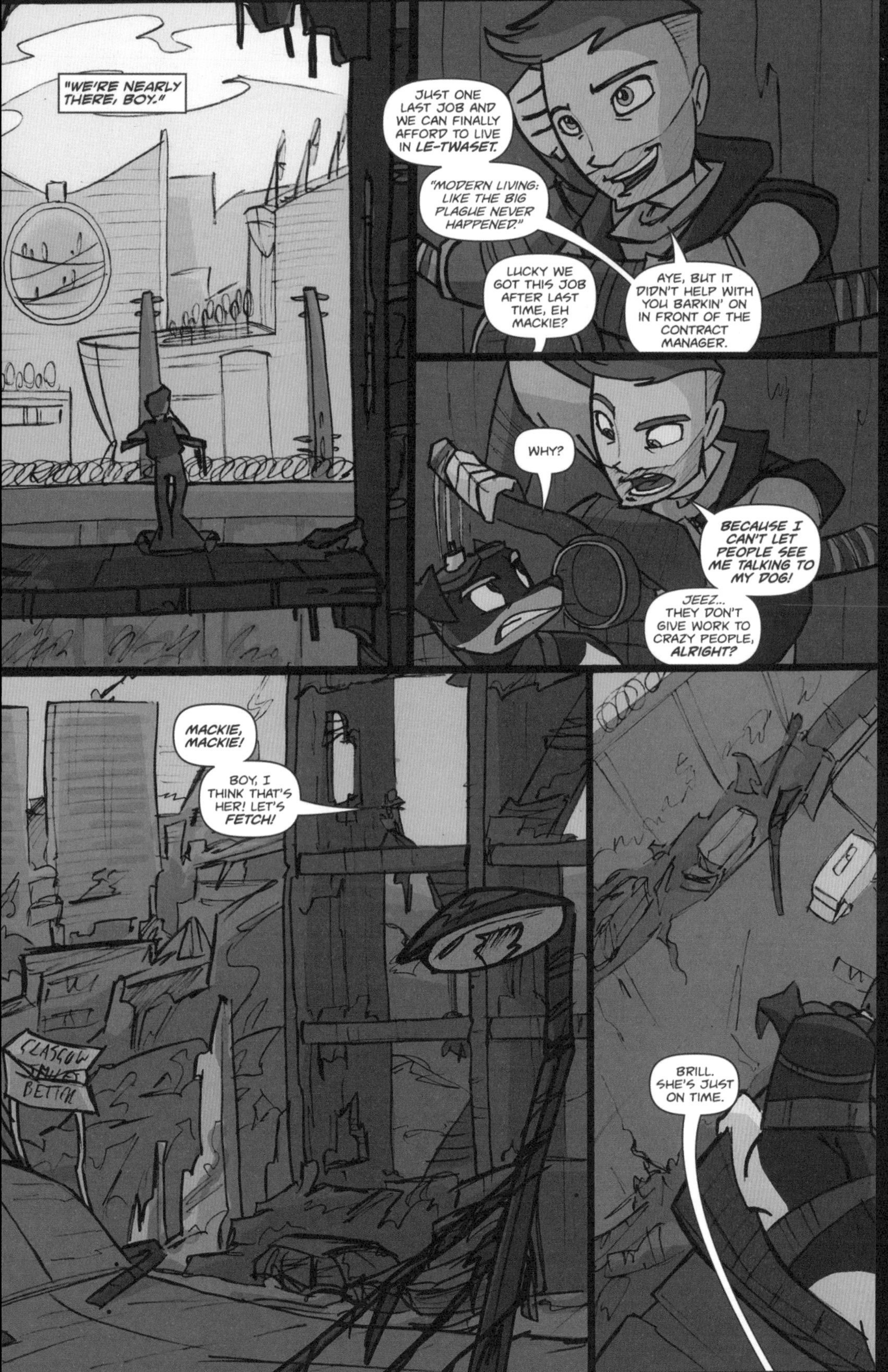
"WE'RE NEARLY THERE, BOY."
JUST ONE LAST JOB AND WE CAN FINALLY AFFORD TO LIVE IN LE-TWASET.
"MODERN LIVING: LIKE THE BIG PLAGUE NEVER HAPPENED."
LUCKY WE GOT THIS JOB AFTER LAST TIME, EH MACKIE?
AYE, BUT IT DIDN'T HELP WITH YOU BARKIN' ON IN FRONT OF THE CONTRACT MANAGER.
WHY?
BECAUSE I CAN'T LET PEOPLE SEE ME TALKING TO MY DOG!
JEEZ... THEY DON'T GIVE WORK TO CRAZY PEOPLE, ALRIGHT?
MACKIE, MACKIE!
BOY, I THINK THAT'S HER! LET'S FETCH!
BRILL. SHE'S JUST ON TIME.

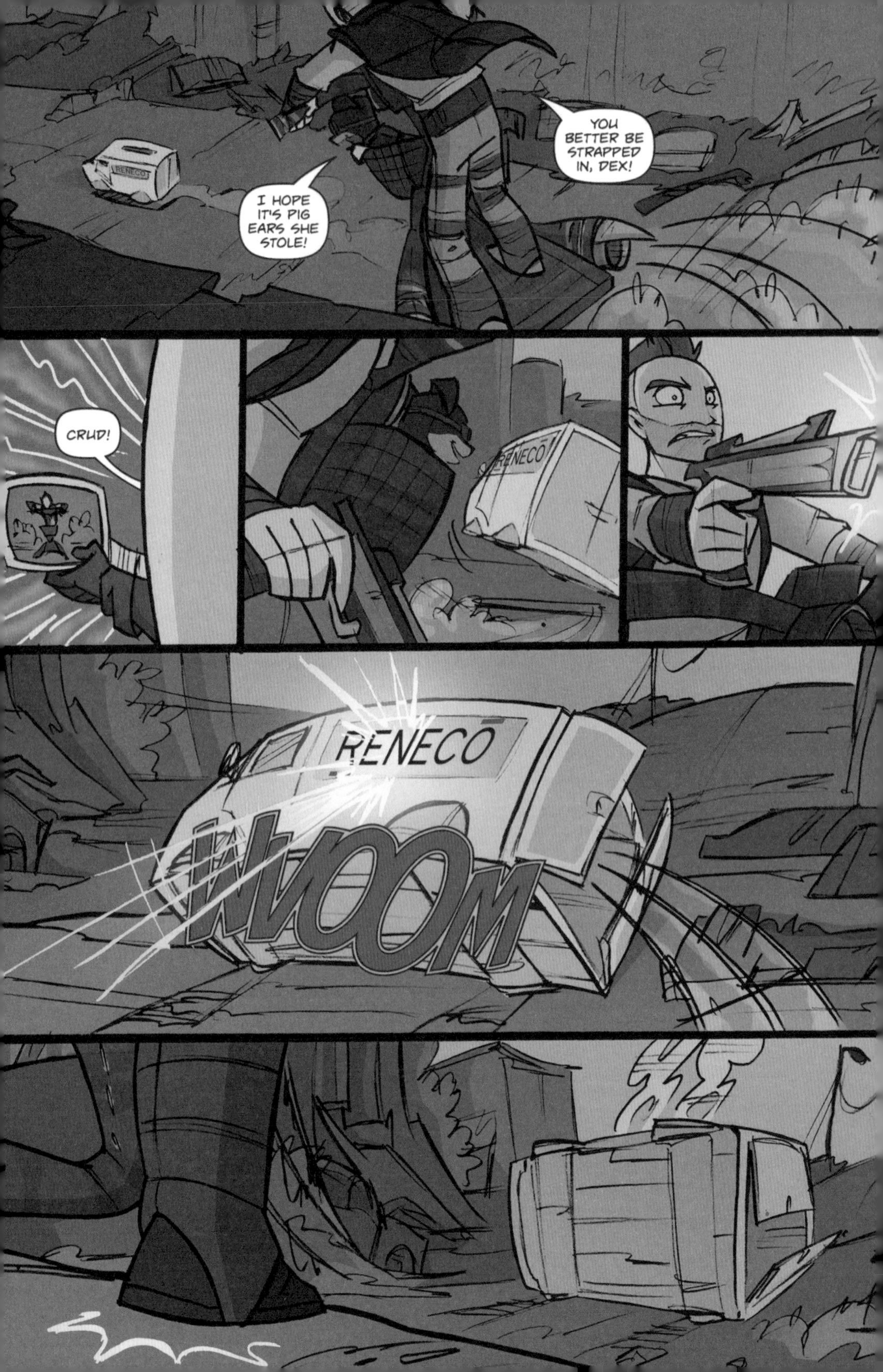
RENECO
I HOPE IT'S PIG EARS SHE STOLE!
YOU BETTER BE STRAPPED IN, DEX!
CRUD!
RENECO
RENECO
WOOM

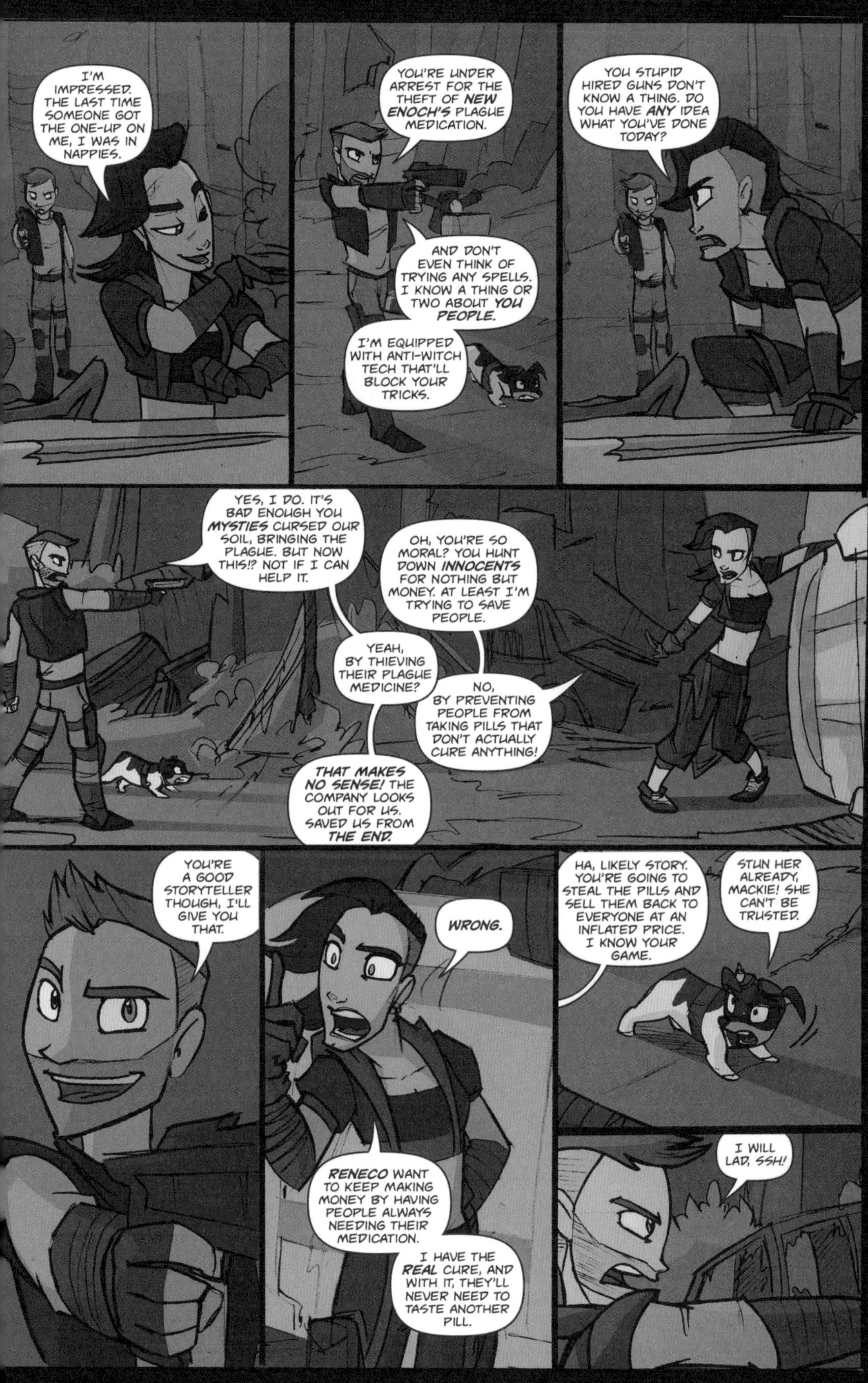

I'M IMPRESSED. THE LAST TIME SOMEONE GOT THE ONE-UP ON ME, I WAS IN NAPPIES.
YOU'RE UNDER ARREST FOR THE THEFT OF NEW ENOCH'S PLAGUE MEDICATION.
AND DON'T EVEN THINK OF TRYING ANY SPELLS. I KNOW A THING OR TWO ABOUT YOU PEOPLE.
I'M EQUIPPED WITH ANTI-WITCH TECH THAT'LL BLOCK YOUR TRICKS.
YOU STUPID HIRED GUNS DON'T KNOW A THING. DO YOU HAVE ANY IDEA WHAT YOU'VE DONE TODAY?
YES, I DO. IT'S BAD ENOUGH YOU MYSTIES CURSED OUR SOIL, BRINGING THE PLAGUE. BUT NOW THIS!? NOT IF I CAN HELP IT.
OH, YOU'RE SO MORAL? YOU HUNT DOWN INNOCENTS FOR NOTHING BUT MONEY. AT LEAST I'M TRYING TO SAVE PEOPLE.
YEAH, BY THIEVING THEIR PLAGUE MEDICINE?
NO, BY PREVENTING PEOPLE FROM TAKING PILLS THAT DON'T ACTUALLY CURE ANYTHING!
THAT MAKES NO SENSE! THE COMPANY LOOKS OUT FOR US. SAVED US FROM THE END.
YOU'RE A GOOD STORYTELLER THOUGH, I'LL GIVE YOU THAT.
WRONG.
RENECO WANT TO KEEP MAKING MONEY BY HAVING PEOPLE ALWAYS NEEDING THEIR MEDICATION.
I HAVE THE REAL CURE, AND WITH IT, THEY'LL NEVER NEED TO TASTE ANOTHER PILL.
HA, LIKELY STORY. YOU'RE GOING TO STEAL THE PILLS AND SELL THEM BACK TO EVERYONE AT AN INFLATED PRICE. I KNOW YOUR GAME.
STUN HER ALREADY, MACKIE! SHE CAN'T BE TRUSTED.
I WILL LAD, SSH!

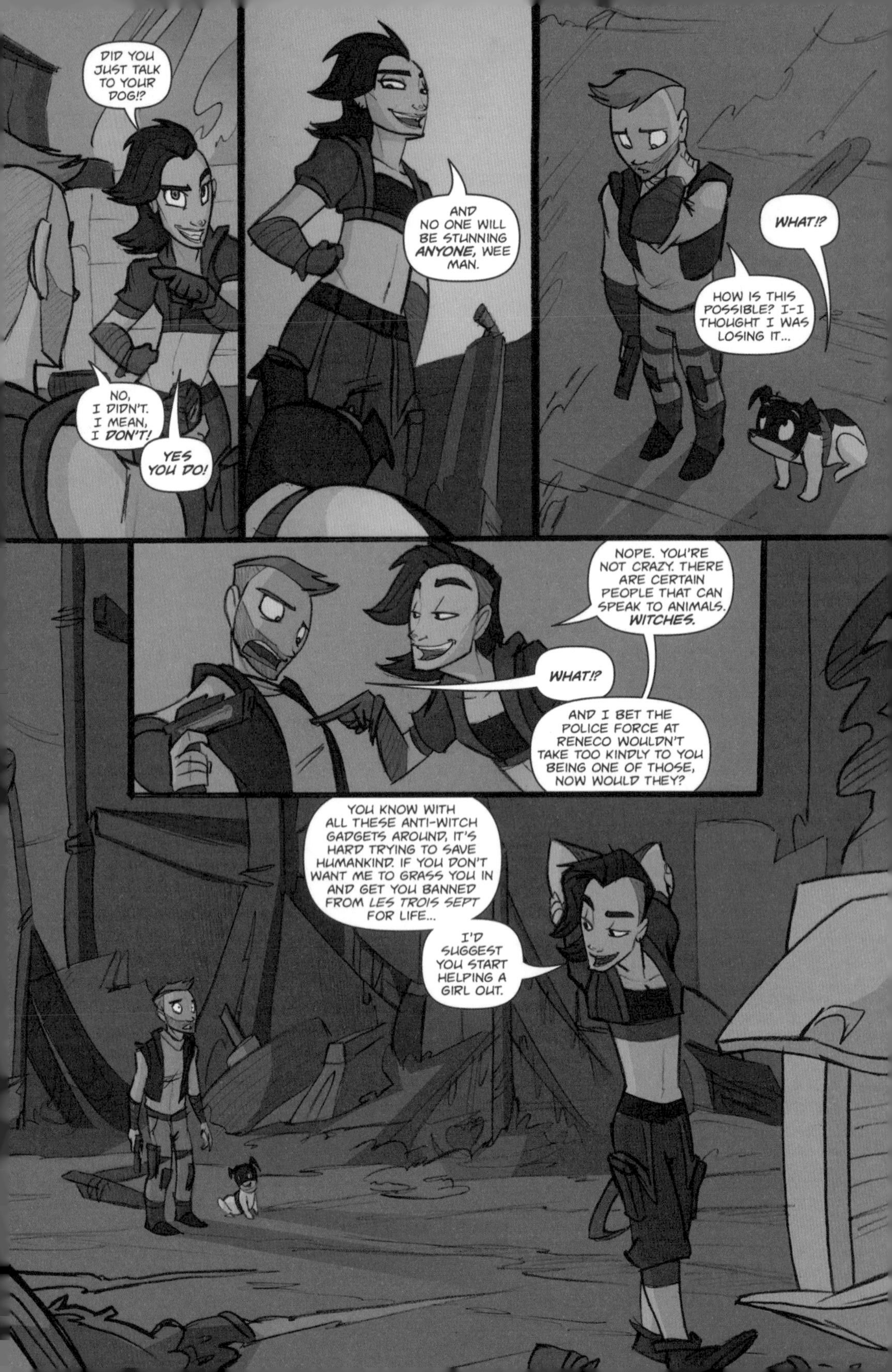
DID YOU JUST TALK TO YOUR DOG!?
NO, I DIDN'T. I MEAN, I *DON'T!*
YES YOU DO!
AND NO ONE WILL BE STUNNING *ANYONE,* WEE MAN.
WHAT!?
HOW IS THIS POSSIBLE? I-I THOUGHT I WAS LOSING IT...
NOPE. YOU'RE NOT CRAZY. THERE ARE CERTAIN PEOPLE THAT CAN SPEAK TO ANIMALS. ***WITCHES.***
WHAT!?
AND I BET THE POLICE FORCE AT RENECO WOULDN'T TAKE TOO KINDLY TO YOU BEING ONE OF THOSE, NOW WOULD THEY?
YOU KNOW WITH ALL THESE ANTI-WITCH GADGETS AROUND, IT'S HARD TRYING TO SAVE HUMANKIND. IF YOU DON'T WANT ME TO GRASS YOU IN AND GET YOU BANNED FROM *LES TROIS SEPT* FOR LIFE...
I'D SUGGEST YOU START HELPING A GIRL OUT.

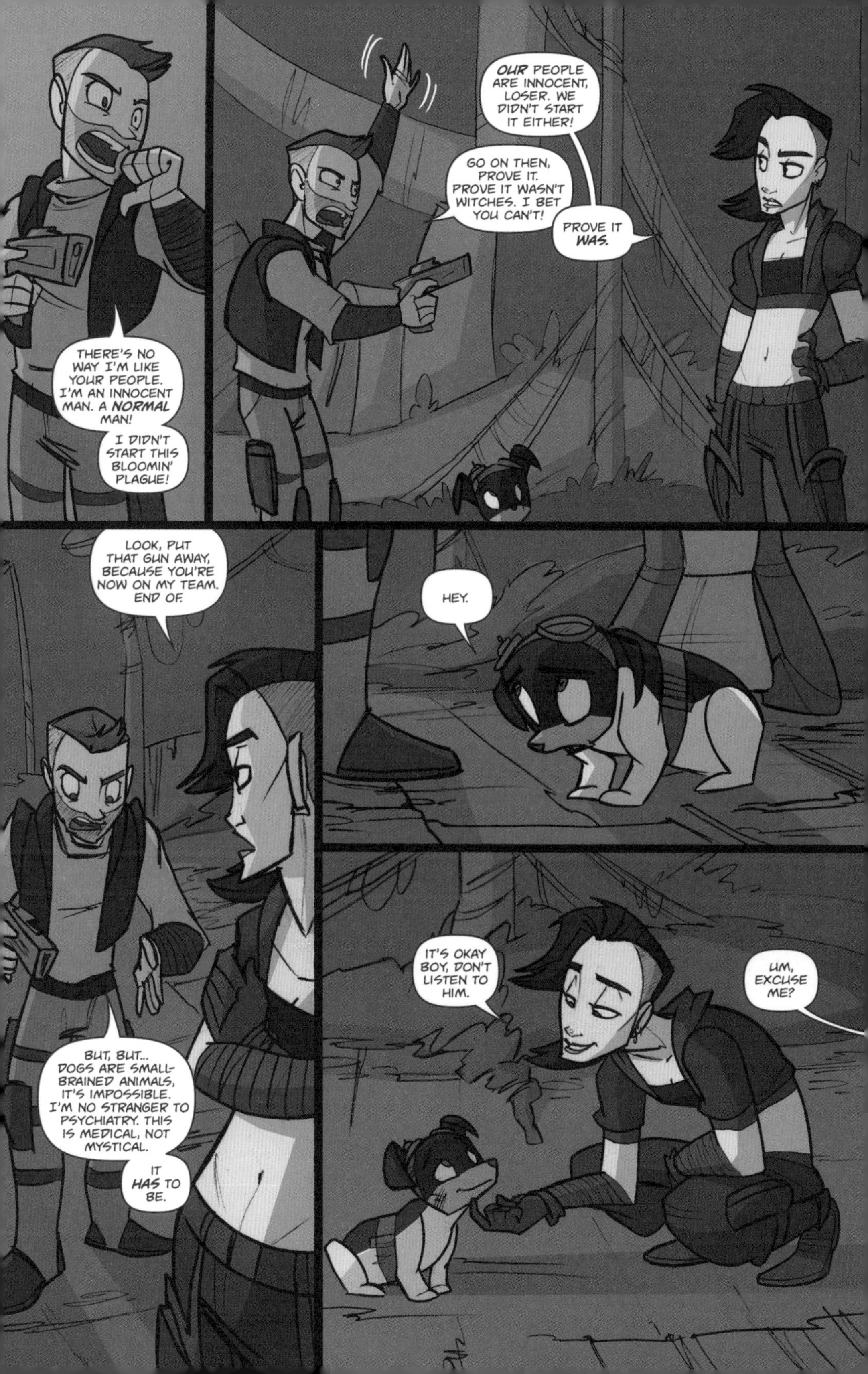

THERE'S NO WAY I'M LIKE YOUR PEOPLE. I'M AN INNOCENT MAN. A **NORMAL** MAN!
I DIDN'T START THIS BLOOMIN' PLAGUE!
OUR PEOPLE ARE INNOCENT, LOSER. WE DIDN'T START IT EITHER!
GO ON THEN, PROVE IT. PROVE IT WASN'T WITCHES. I BET YOU CAN'T!
PROVE IT **WAS.**
LOOK, PUT THAT GUN AWAY, BECAUSE YOU'RE NOW ON MY TEAM. END OF.
BUT, BUT... DOGS ARE SMALL-BRAINED ANIMALS, IT'S IMPOSSIBLE. I'M NO STRANGER TO PSYCHIATRY. THIS IS MEDICAL, NOT MYSTICAL.
IT **HAS** TO BE.
HEY.
IT'S OKAY BOY, DON'T LISTEN TO HIM.
UM, EXCUSE ME?

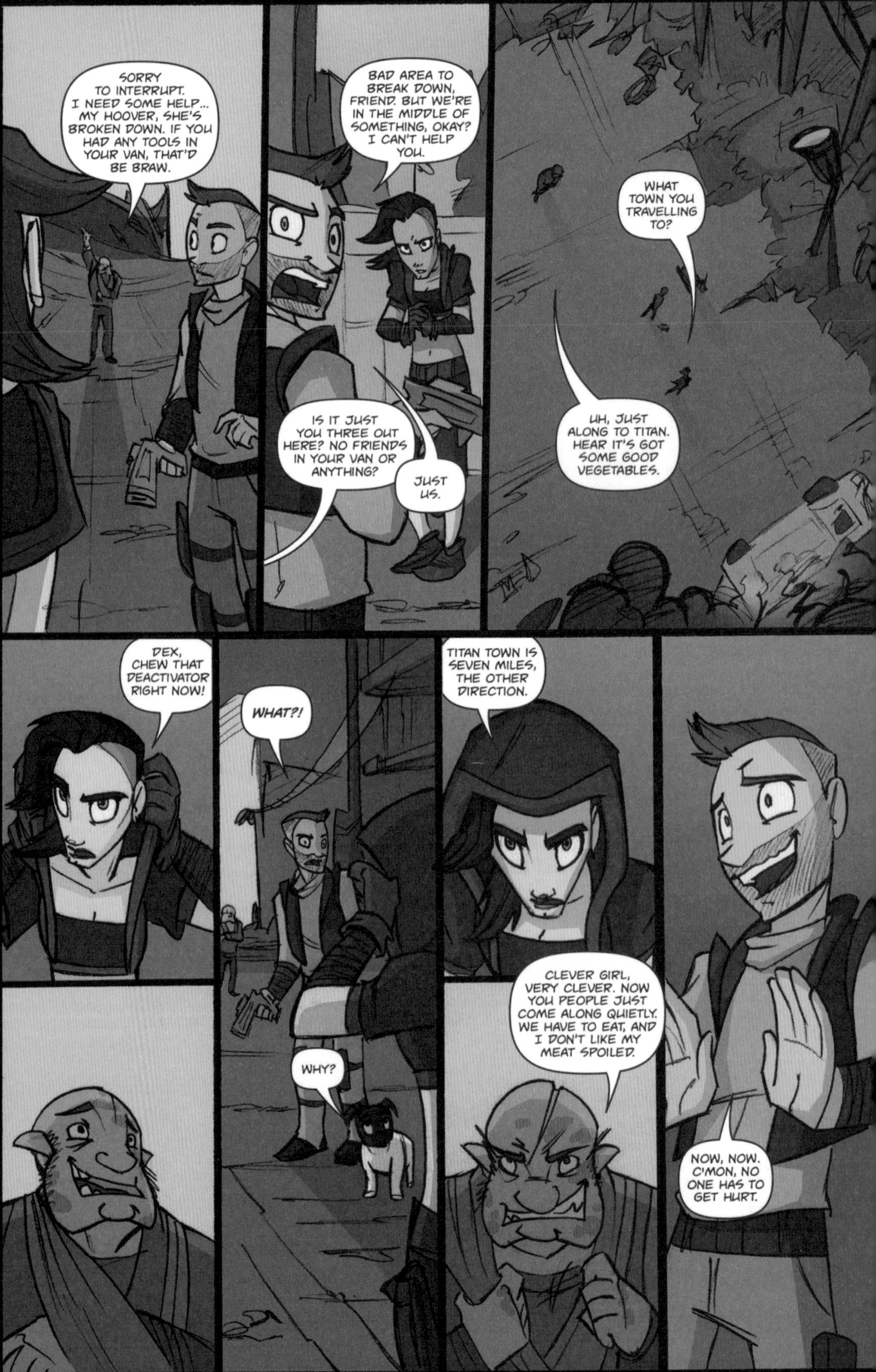
SORRY TO INTERRUPT. I NEED SOME HELP... MY HOOVER, SHE'S BROKEN DOWN. IF YOU HAD ANY TOOLS IN YOUR VAN, THAT'D BE BRAW.
BAD AREA TO BREAK DOWN, FRIEND. BUT WE'RE IN THE MIDDLE OF SOMETHING, OKAY? I CAN'T HELP YOU.
IS IT JUST YOU THREE OUT HERE? NO FRIENDS IN YOUR VAN OR ANYTHING?
JUST US.
WHAT TOWN YOU TRAVELLING TO?
UH, JUST ALONG TO TITAN. HEAR IT'S GOT SOME GOOD VEGETABLES.
DEX, CHEW THAT DEACTIVATOR RIGHT NOW!
WHAT?!
WHY?
TITAN TOWN IS SEVEN MILES, THE OTHER DIRECTION.
CLEVER GIRL, VERY CLEVER. NOW YOU PEOPLE JUST COME ALONG QUIETLY. WE HAVE TO EAT, AND I DON'T LIKE MY MEAT SPOILED.
NOW, NOW. C'MON, NO ONE HAS TO GET HURT.

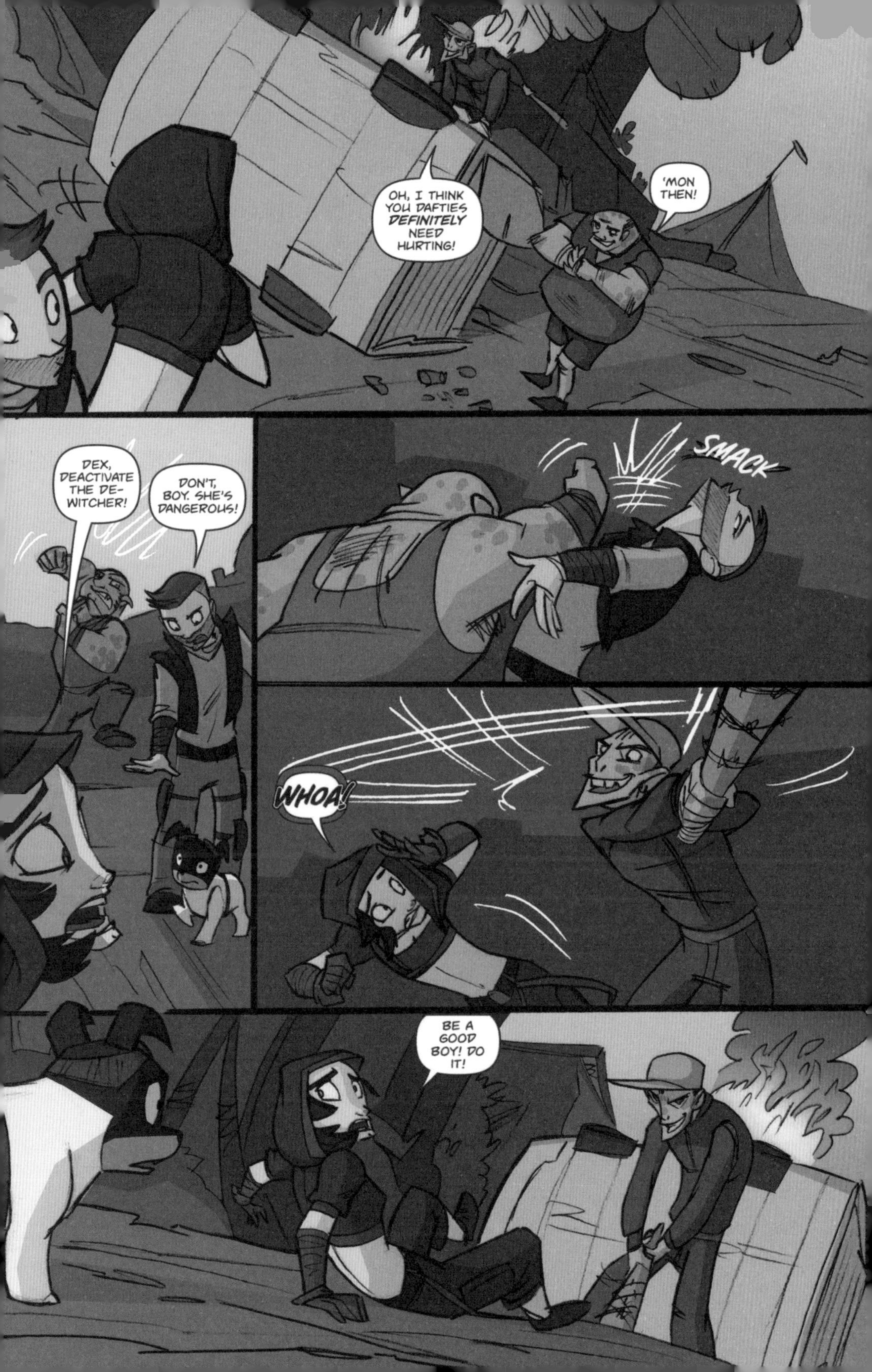
OH, I THINK YOU DAFTIES DEFINITELY NEED HURTING!
'MON THEN!
DEX, DEACTIVATE THE DE-WITCHER!
DON'T, BOY. SHE'S DANGEROUS!
SMACK
WHOA!
BE A GOOD BOY! DO IT!

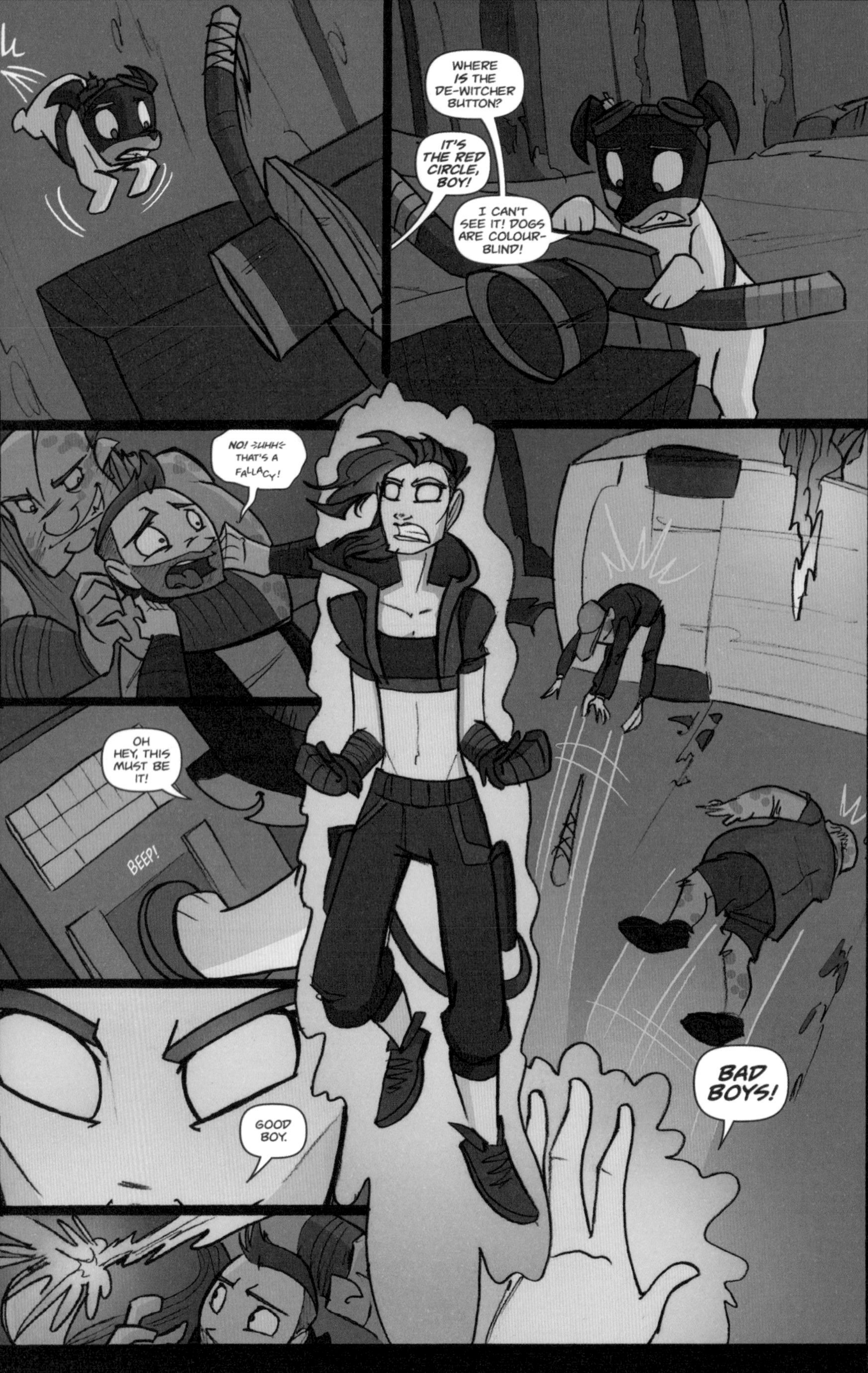
WHERE IS THE DE-WITCHER BUTTON?
IT'S THE RED CIRCLE, BOY!
I CAN'T SEE IT! DOGS ARE COLOUR-BLIND!
NO! UHH THAT'S A FALLACY!
OH HEY, THIS MUST BE IT!
BEEP!
GOOD BOY.
BAD BOYS!

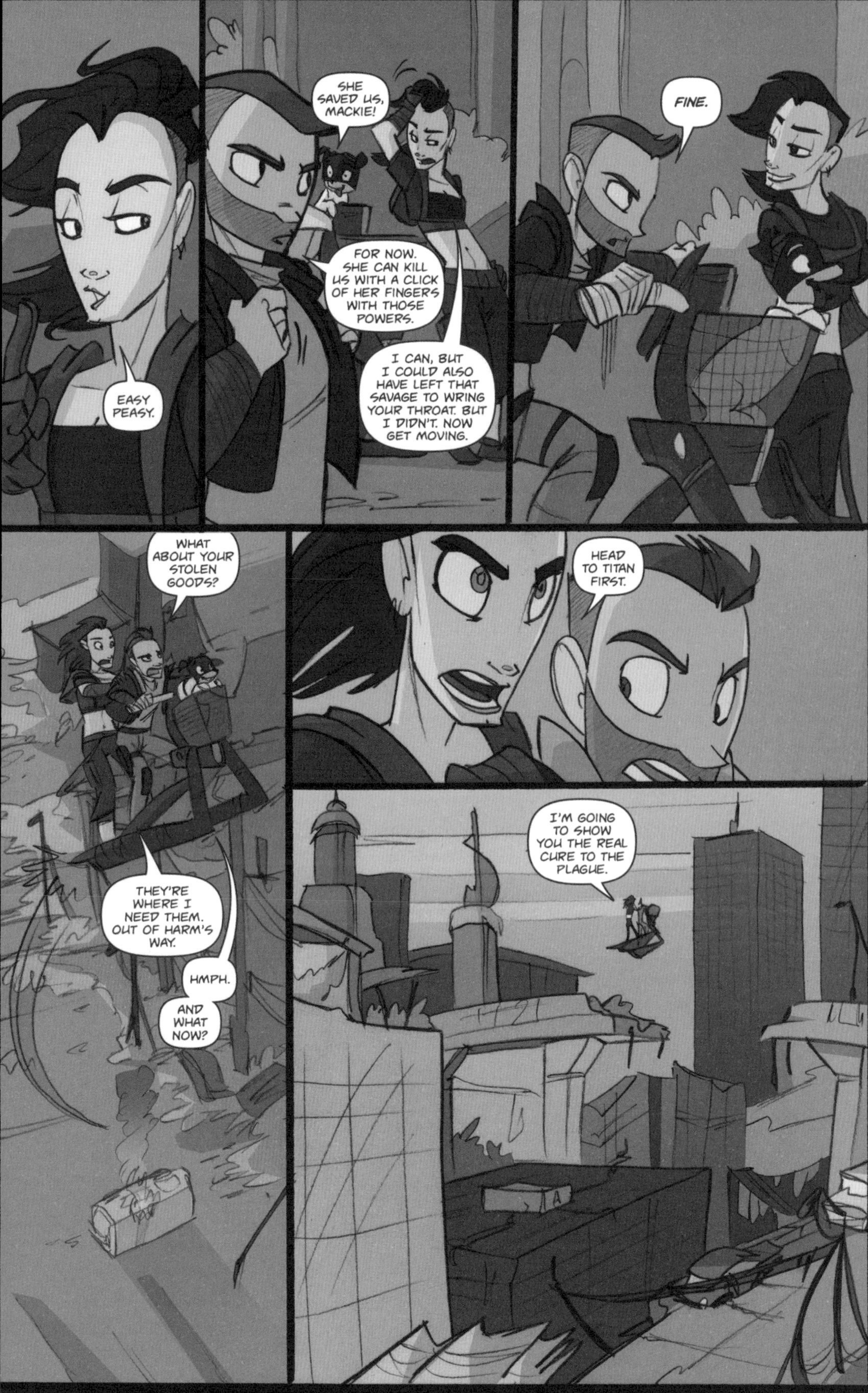
EASY PEASY.
SHE SAVED US, MACKIE!
FOR NOW. SHE CAN KILL US WITH A CLICK OF HER FINGERS WITH THOSE POWERS.
I CAN, BUT I COULD ALSO HAVE LEFT THAT SAVAGE TO WRING YOUR THROAT. BUT I DIDN'T. NOW GET MOVING.
FINE.
WHAT ABOUT YOUR STOLEN GOODS?
THEY'RE WHERE I NEED THEM. OUT OF HARM'S WAY.
HMPH.
AND WHAT NOW?
HEAD TO TITAN FIRST.
I'M GOING TO SHOW YOU THE REAL CURE TO THE PLAGUE.

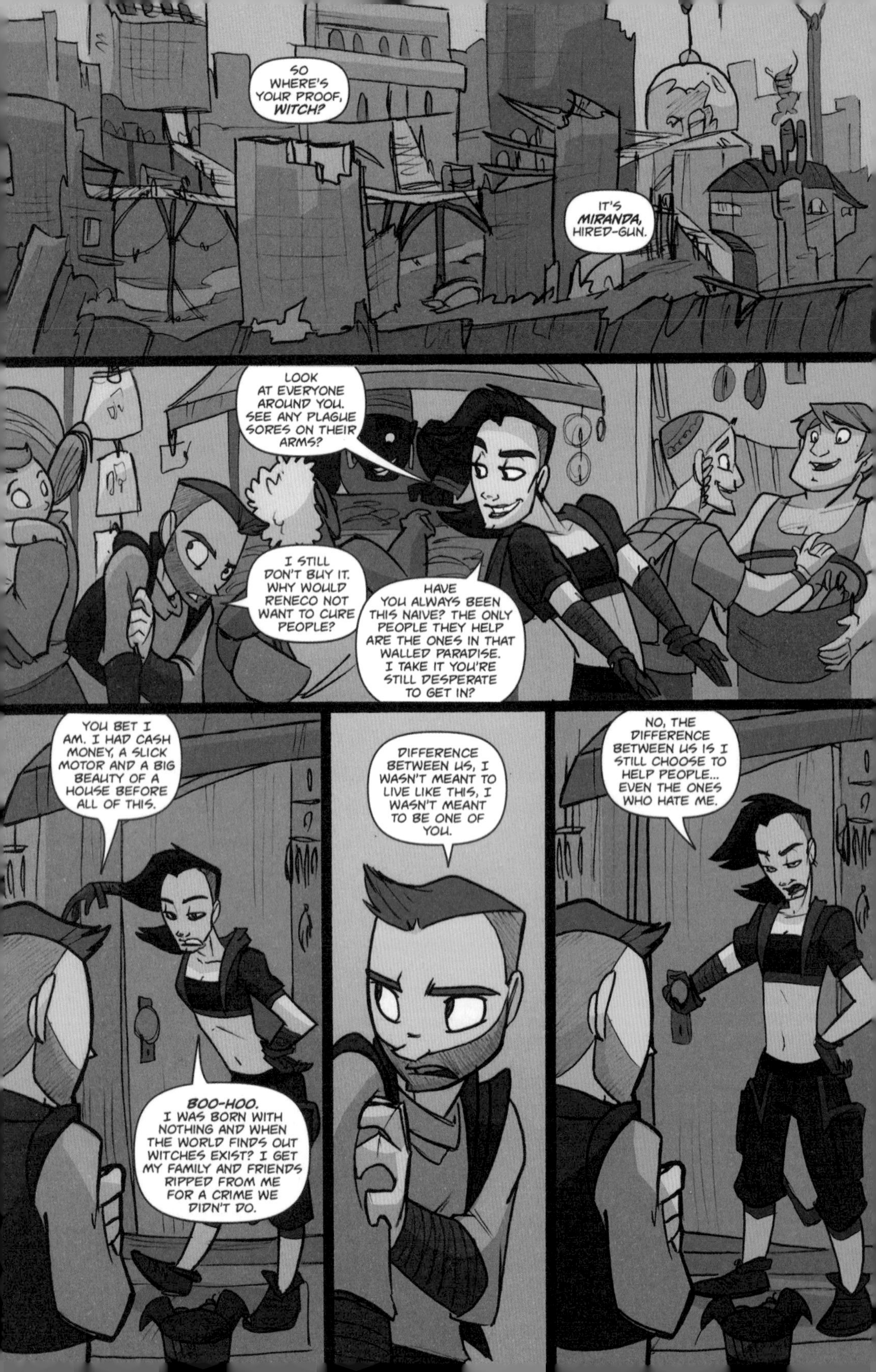
SO WHERE'S YOUR PROOF, WITCH?
IT'S MIRANDA, HIRED-GUN.
LOOK AT EVERYONE AROUND YOU. SEE ANY PLAGUE SORES ON THEIR ARMS?
I STILL DON'T BUY IT. WHY WOULD RENECO NOT WANT TO CURE PEOPLE?
HAVE YOU ALWAYS BEEN THIS NAIVE? THE ONLY PEOPLE THEY HELP ARE THE ONES IN THAT WALLED PARADISE. I TAKE IT YOU'RE STILL DESPERATE TO GET IN?
YOU BET I AM. I HAD CASH MONEY, A SLICK MOTOR AND A BIG BEAUTY OF A HOUSE BEFORE ALL OF THIS.
BOO-HOO. I WAS BORN WITH NOTHING AND WHEN THE WORLD FINDS OUT WITCHES EXIST? I GET MY FAMILY AND FRIENDS RIPPED FROM ME FOR A CRIME WE DIDN'T DO.
DIFFERENCE BETWEEN US, I WASN'T MEANT TO LIVE LIKE THIS, I WASN'T MEANT TO BE ONE OF YOU.
NO, THE DIFFERENCE BETWEEN US IS I STILL CHOOSE TO HELP PEOPLE... EVEN THE ONES WHO HATE ME.

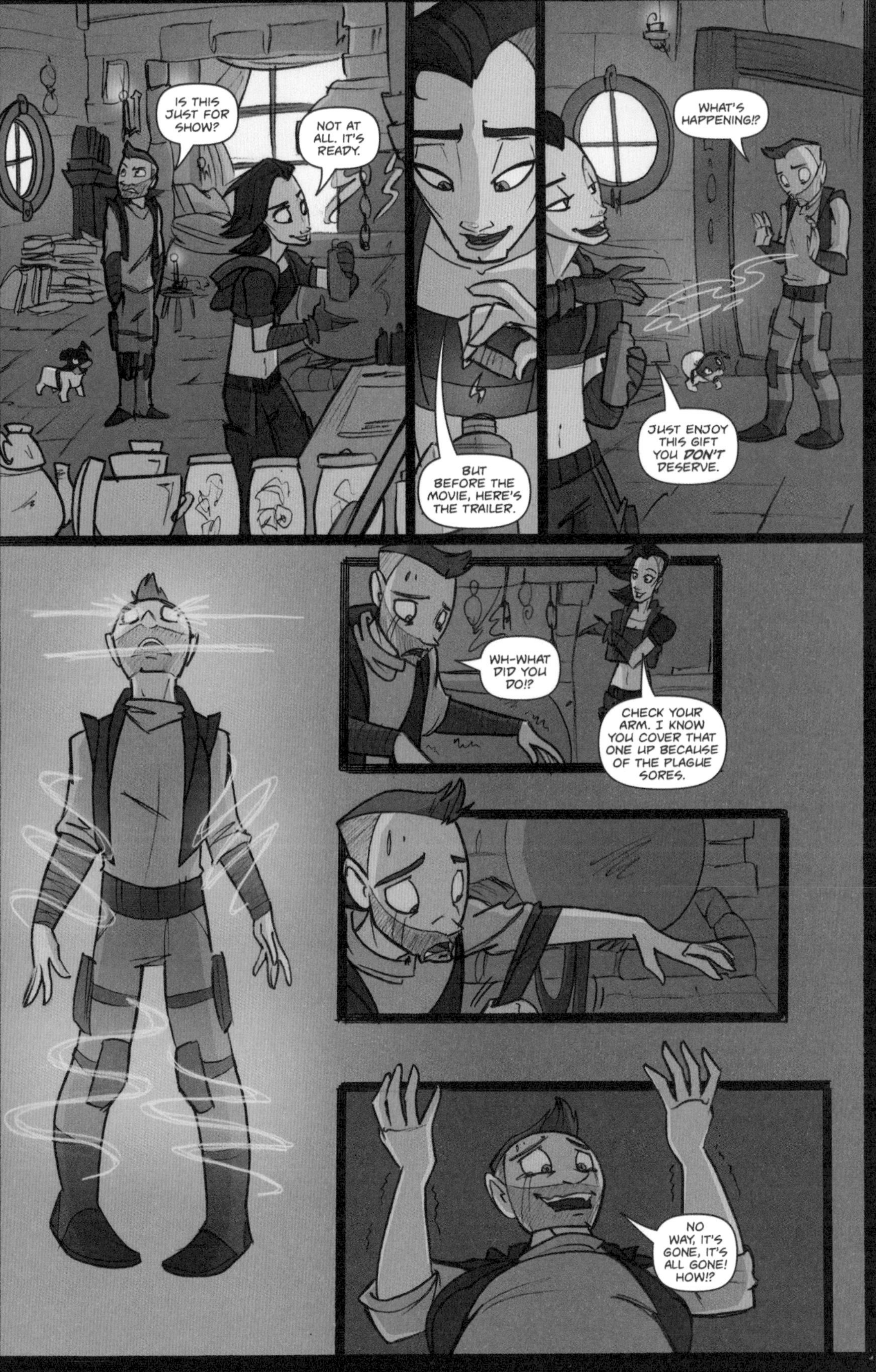
IS THIS JUST FOR SHOW?
NOT AT ALL. IT'S READY.
BUT BEFORE THE MOVIE, HERE'S THE TRAILER.
WHAT'S HAPPENING!?
JUST ENJOY THIS GIFT YOU DON'T DESERVE.
WH-WHAT DID YOU DO!?
CHECK YOUR ARM. I KNOW YOU COVER THAT ONE UP BECAUSE OF THE PLAGUE SORES.
NO WAY, IT'S GONE, IT'S ALL GONE! HOW!?

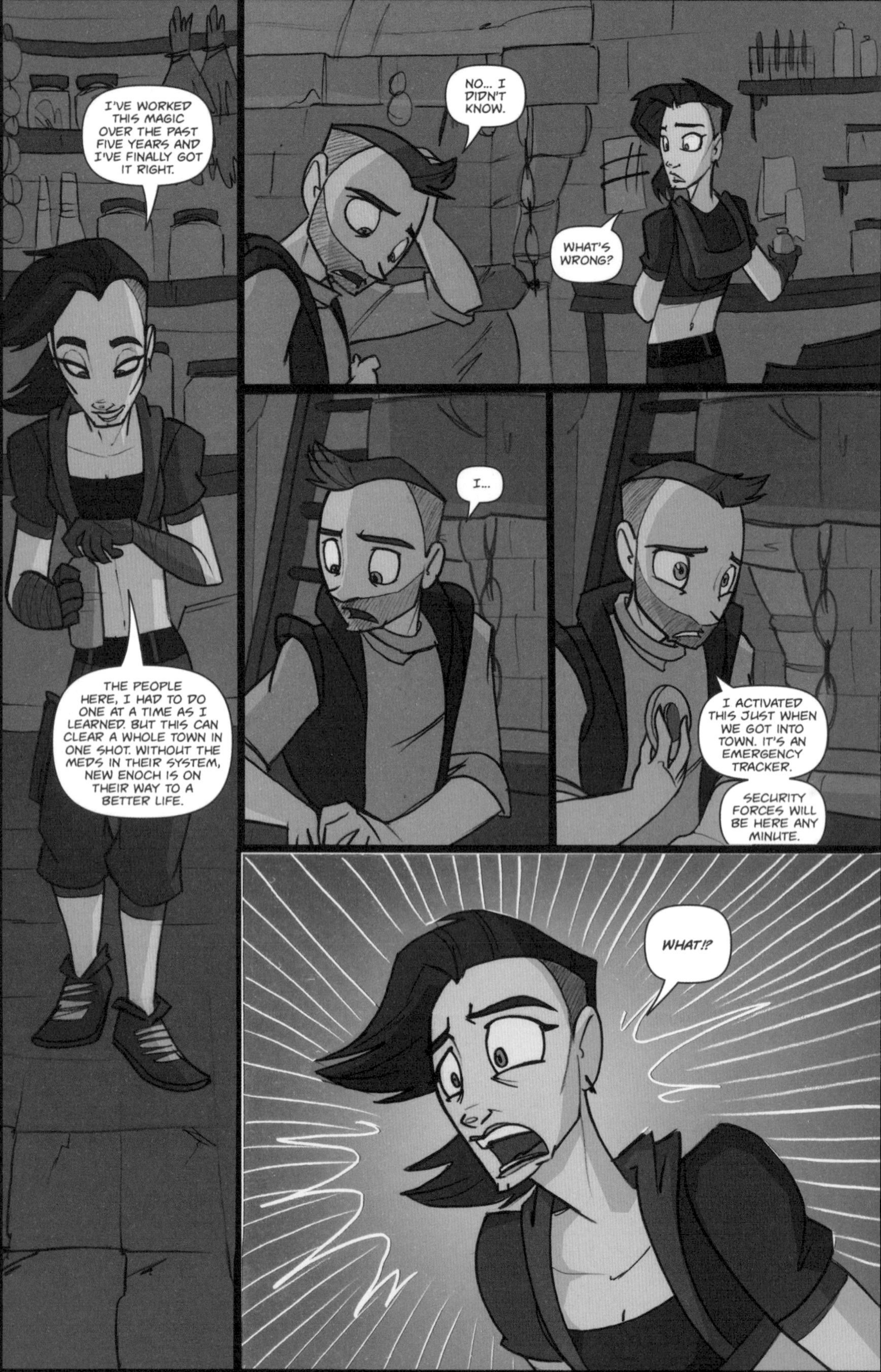
I'VE WORKED THIS MAGIC OVER THE PAST FIVE YEARS AND I'VE FINALLY GOT IT RIGHT.
THE PEOPLE HERE, I HAD TO DO ONE AT A TIME AS I LEARNED. BUT THIS CAN CLEAR A WHOLE TOWN IN ONE SHOT. WITHOUT THE MEDS IN THEIR SYSTEM, NEW ENOCH IS ON THEIR WAY TO A BETTER LIFE.
NO... I DIDN'T KNOW.
WHAT'S WRONG?
I...
I ACTIVATED THIS JUST WHEN WE GOT INTO TOWN. IT'S AN EMERGENCY TRACKER.
SECURITY FORCES WILL BE HERE ANY MINUTE.
WHAT!?

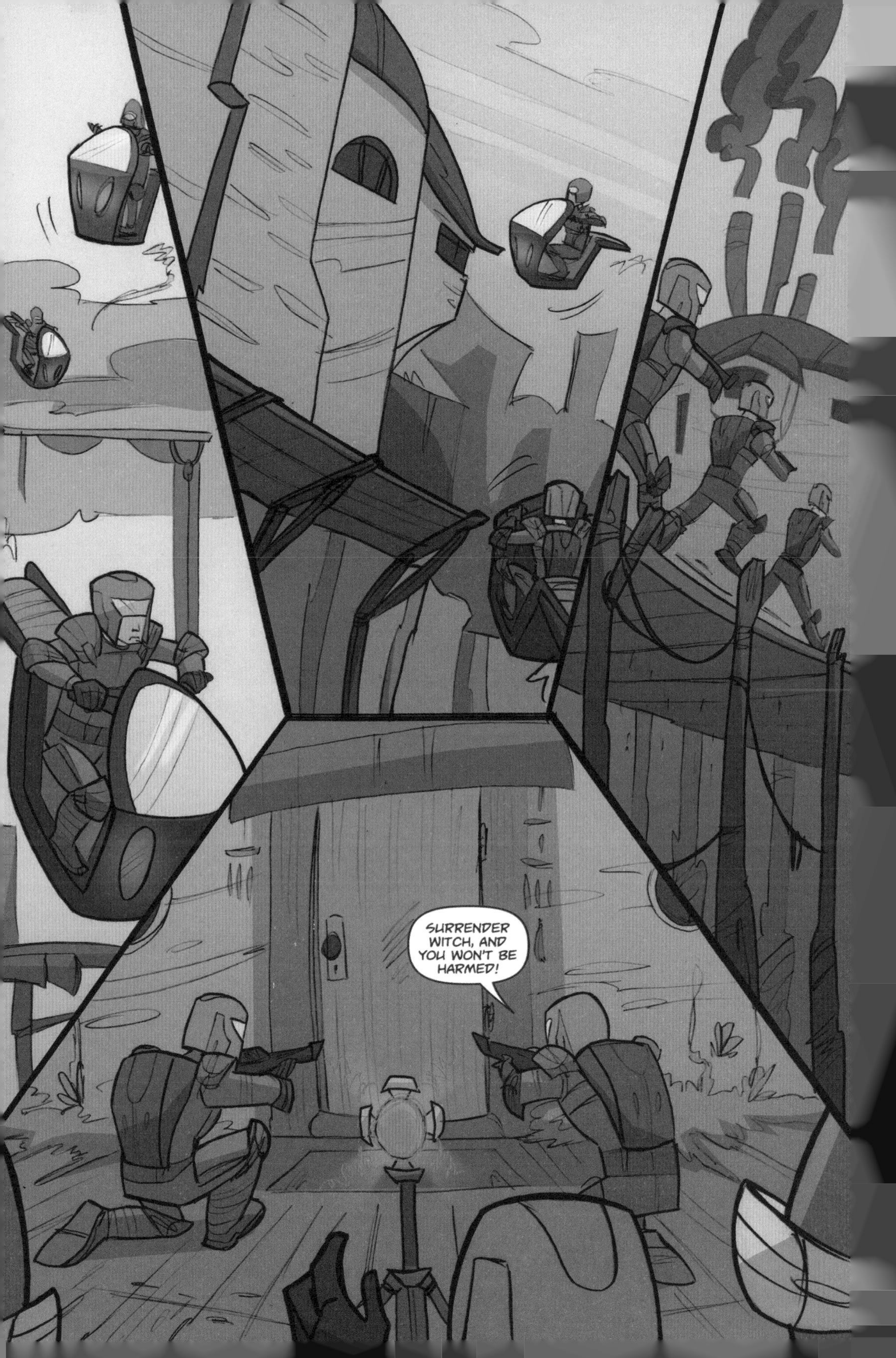
SURRENDER WITCH, AND YOU WON'T BE HARMED!

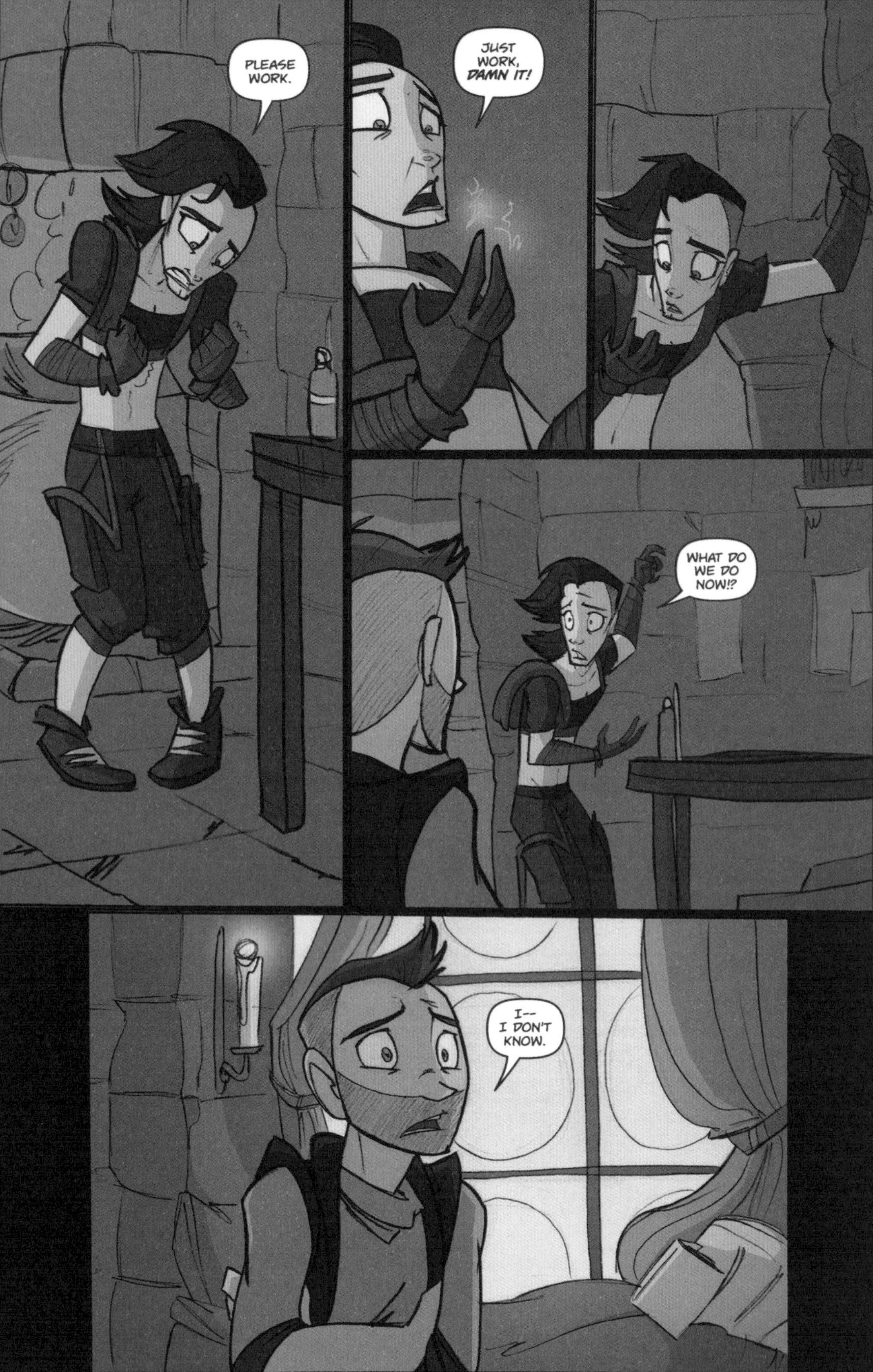
PLEASE WORK.
JUST WORK, *DAMN IT!*
WHAT DO WE DO NOW!?
I-- I DON'T KNOW.

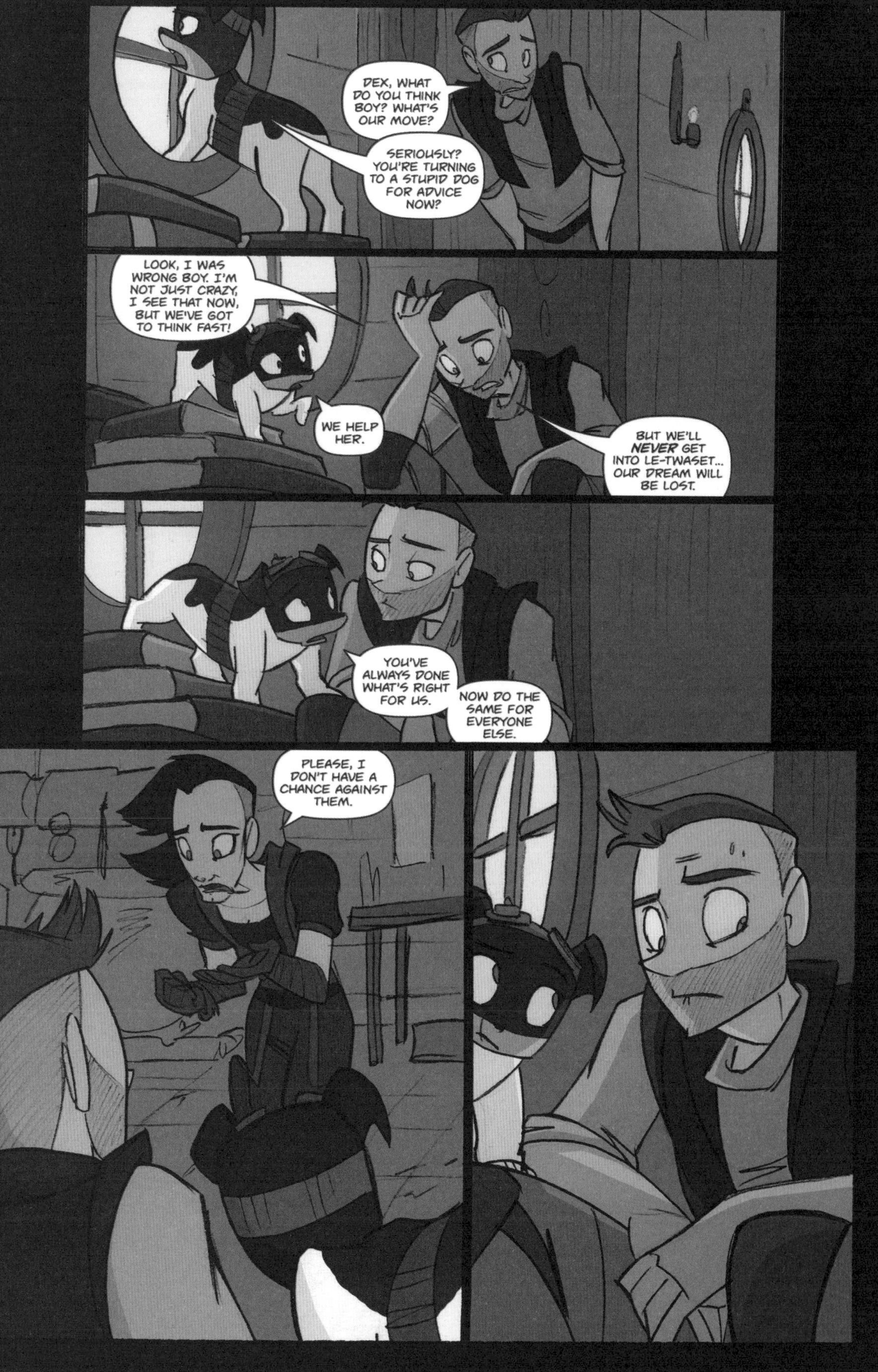
DEX, WHAT DO YOU THINK BOY? WHAT'S OUR MOVE?
SERIOUSLY? YOU'RE TURNING TO A STUPID DOG FOR ADVICE NOW?
LOOK, I WAS WRONG BOY. I'M NOT JUST CRAZY, I SEE THAT NOW, BUT WE'VE GOT TO THINK FAST!
WE HELP HER.
BUT WE'LL NEVER GET INTO LE-TWASET... OUR DREAM WILL BE LOST.
YOU'VE ALWAYS DONE WHAT'S RIGHT FOR US.
NOW DO THE SAME FOR EVERYONE ELSE.
PLEASE, I DON'T HAVE A CHANCE AGAINST THEM.

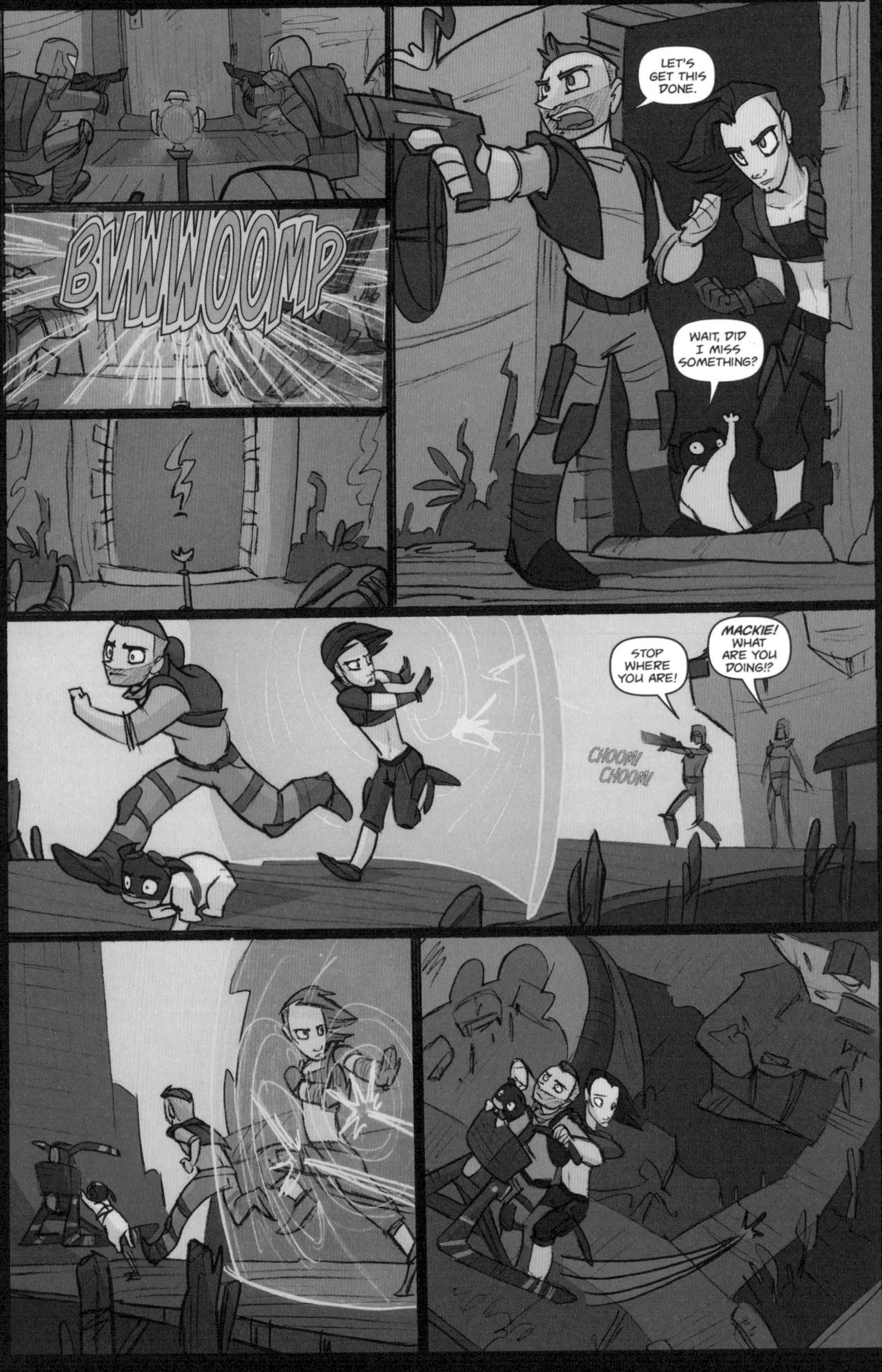

LET'S GET THIS DONE.
BVWWOOMP
WAIT, DID I MISS SOMETHING?
MACKIE! WHAT ARE YOU DOING!?
STOP WHERE YOU ARE!
CHOOM! CHOOM!

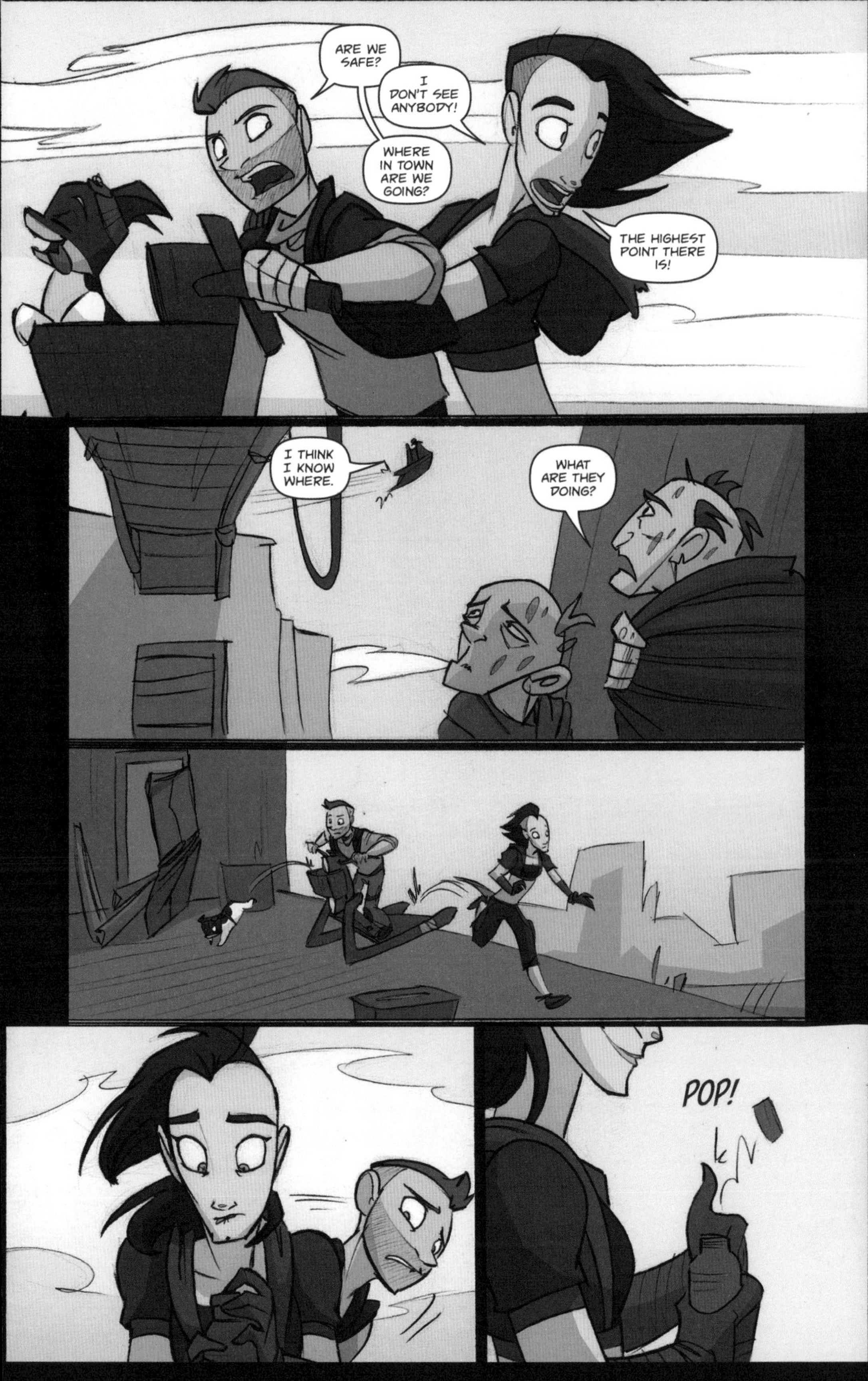
ARE WE SAFE?
I DON'T SEE ANYBODY!
WHERE IN TOWN ARE WE GOING?
THE HIGHEST POINT THERE IS!
I THINK I KNOW WHERE.
WHAT ARE THEY DOING?
POP!

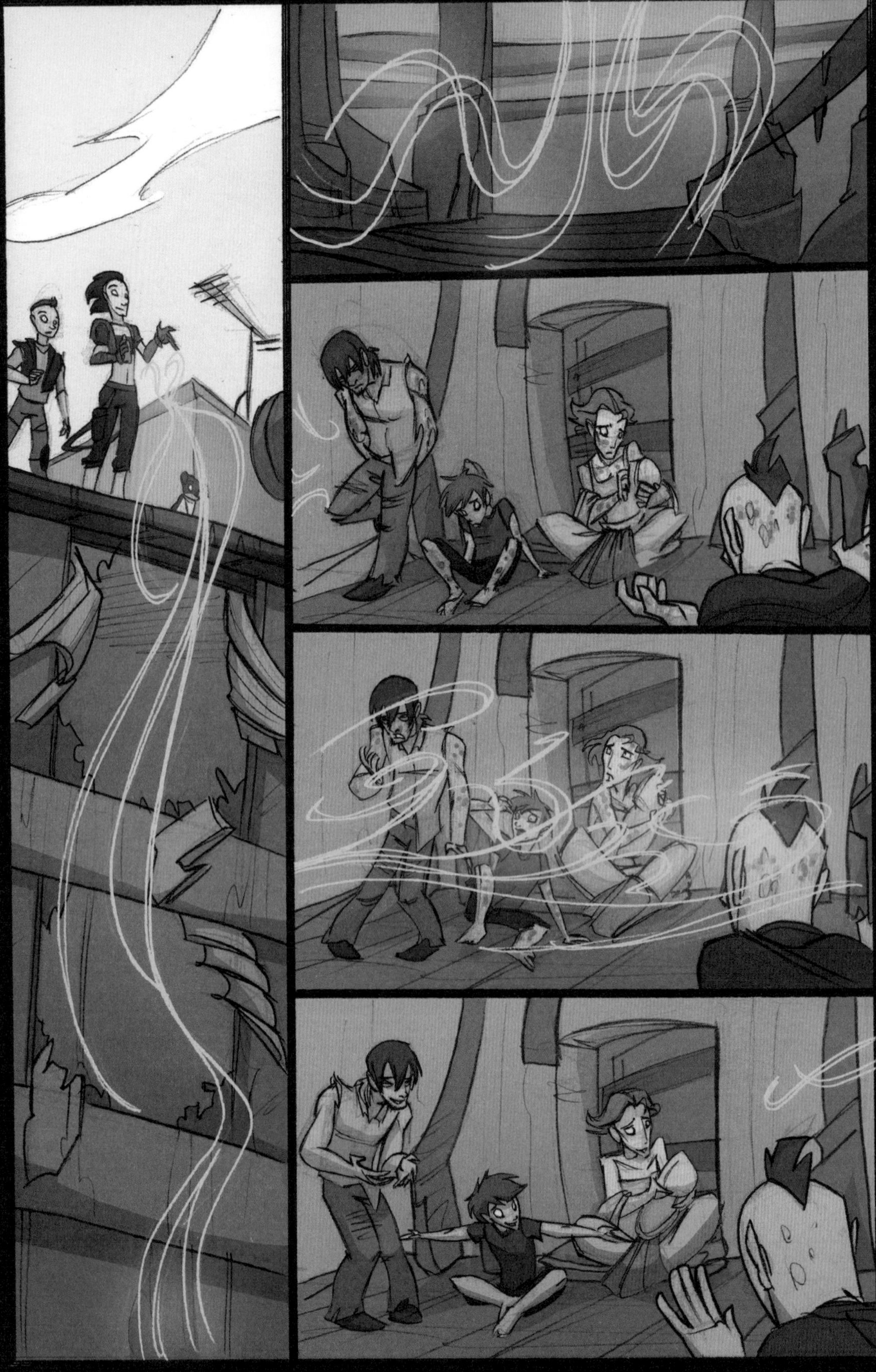

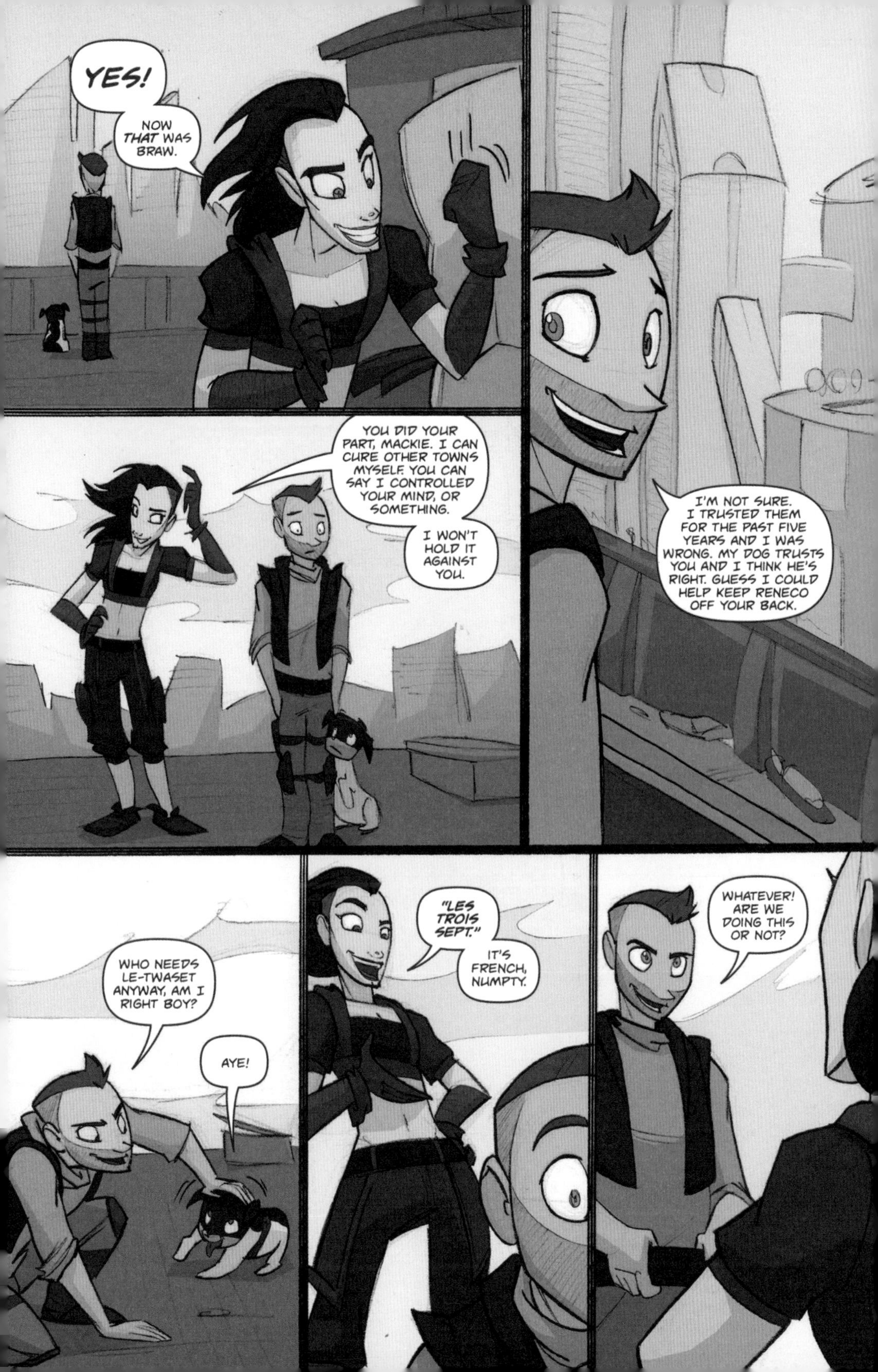
YES!
NOW *THAT* WAS BRAW.
YOU DID YOUR PART, MACKIE. I CAN CURE OTHER TOWNS MYSELF. YOU CAN SAY I CONTROLLED YOUR MIND, OR SOMETHING.
I WON'T HOLD IT AGAINST YOU.
I'M NOT SURE. I TRUSTED THEM FOR THE PAST FIVE YEARS AND I WAS WRONG. MY DOG TRUSTS YOU AND I THINK HE'S RIGHT. GUESS I COULD HELP KEEP RENECO OFF YOUR BACK.
WHO NEEDS LE-TWASET ANYWAY, AM I RIGHT BOY?
AYE!
"LES TROIS SEPT."
IT'S FRENCH, NUMPTY.
WHATEVER! ARE WE DOING THIS OR NOT?

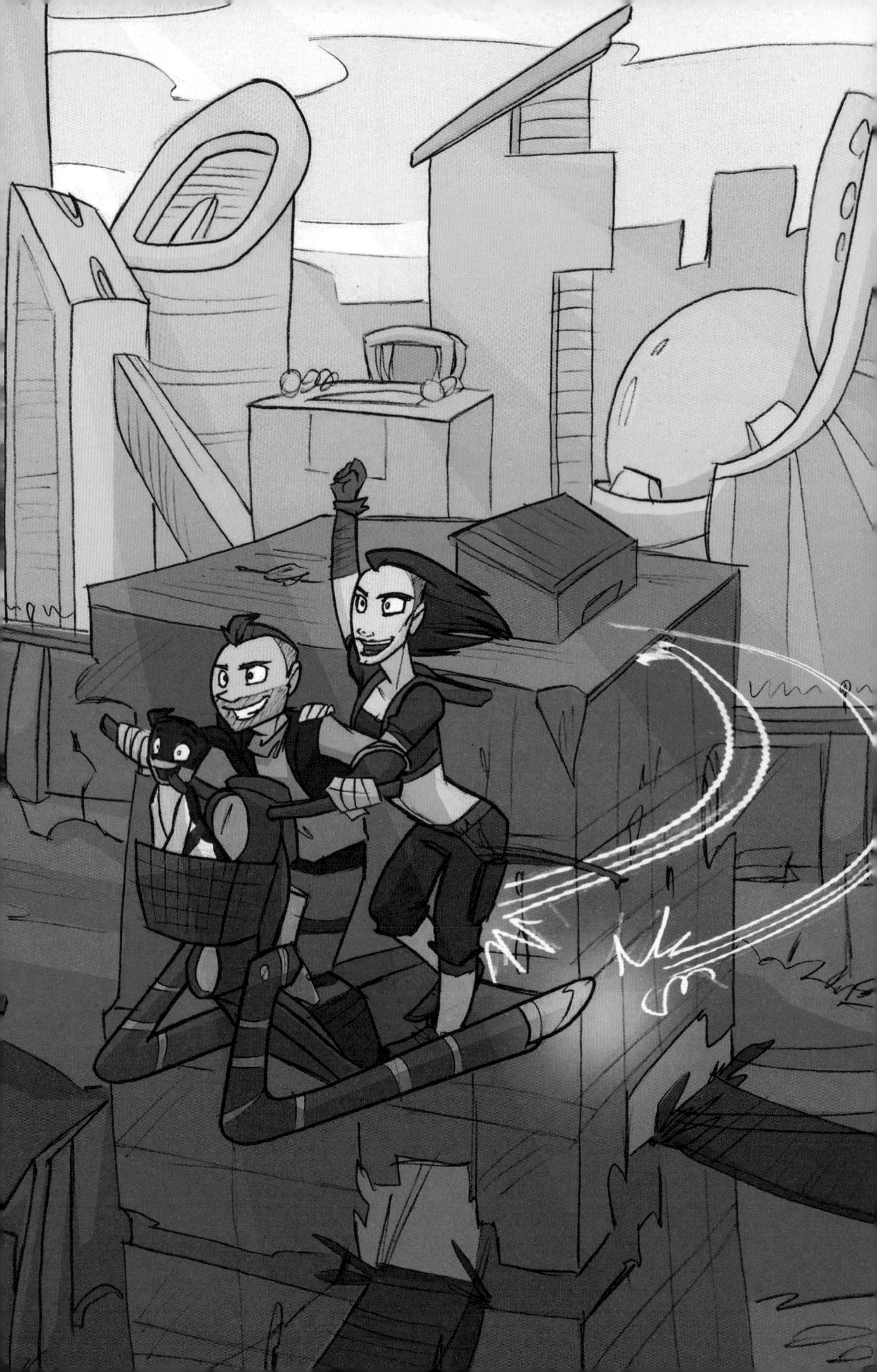

DON'T FORGET TO TAKE YOUR PILL HEN, WE'VE NO GOT MUCH LEFT!
TING
OKAY, MUM!
NO!

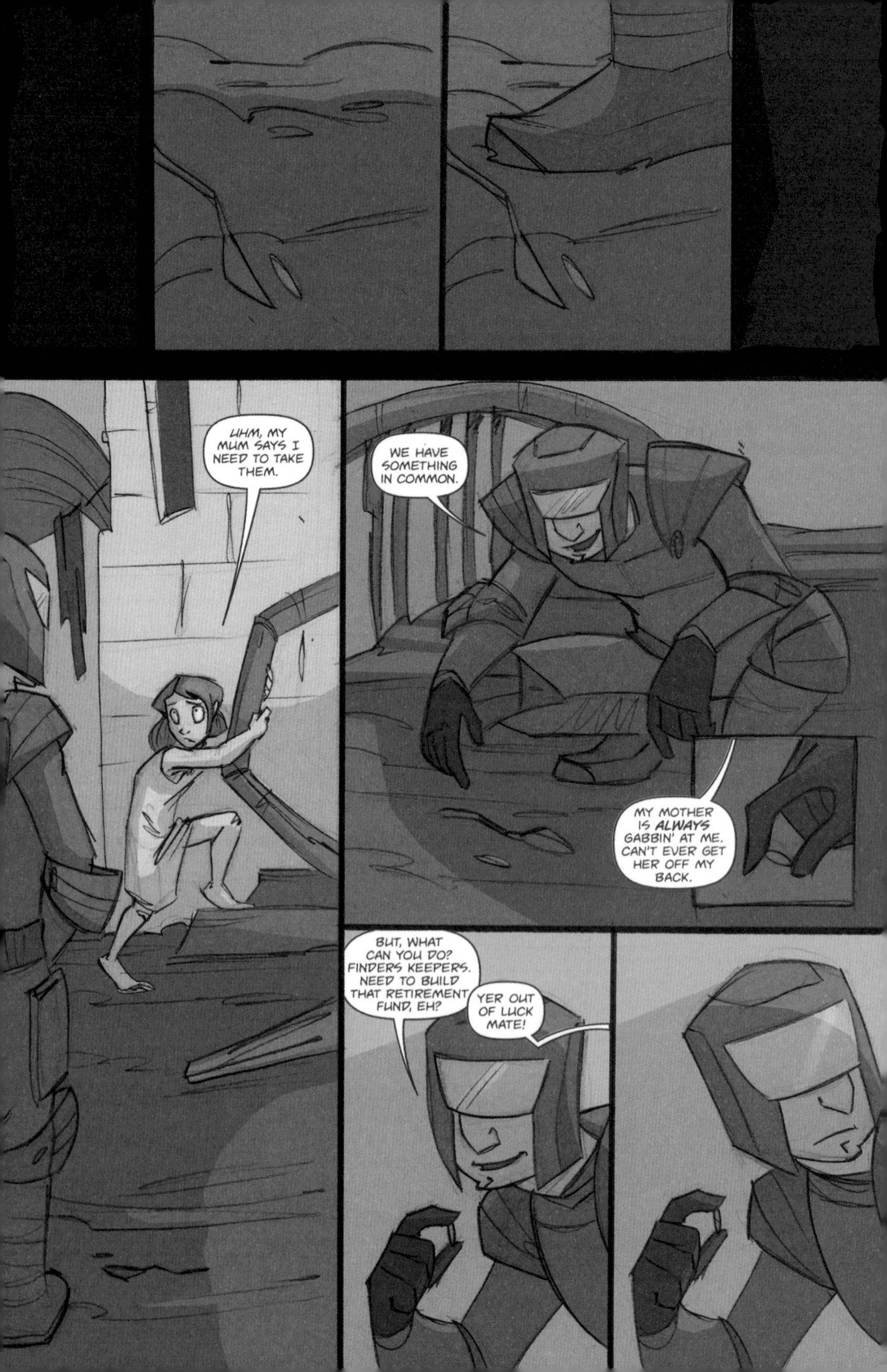
UHM, MY MUM SAYS I NEED TO TAKE THEM.
WE HAVE SOMETHING IN COMMON.
MY MOTHER IS *ALWAYS* GABBIN' AT ME. CAN'T EVER GET HER OFF MY BACK.
BUT, WHAT CAN YOU DO? FINDERS KEEPERS. NEED TO BUILD THAT RETIREMENT FUND, EH?
YER OUT OF LUCK MATE!

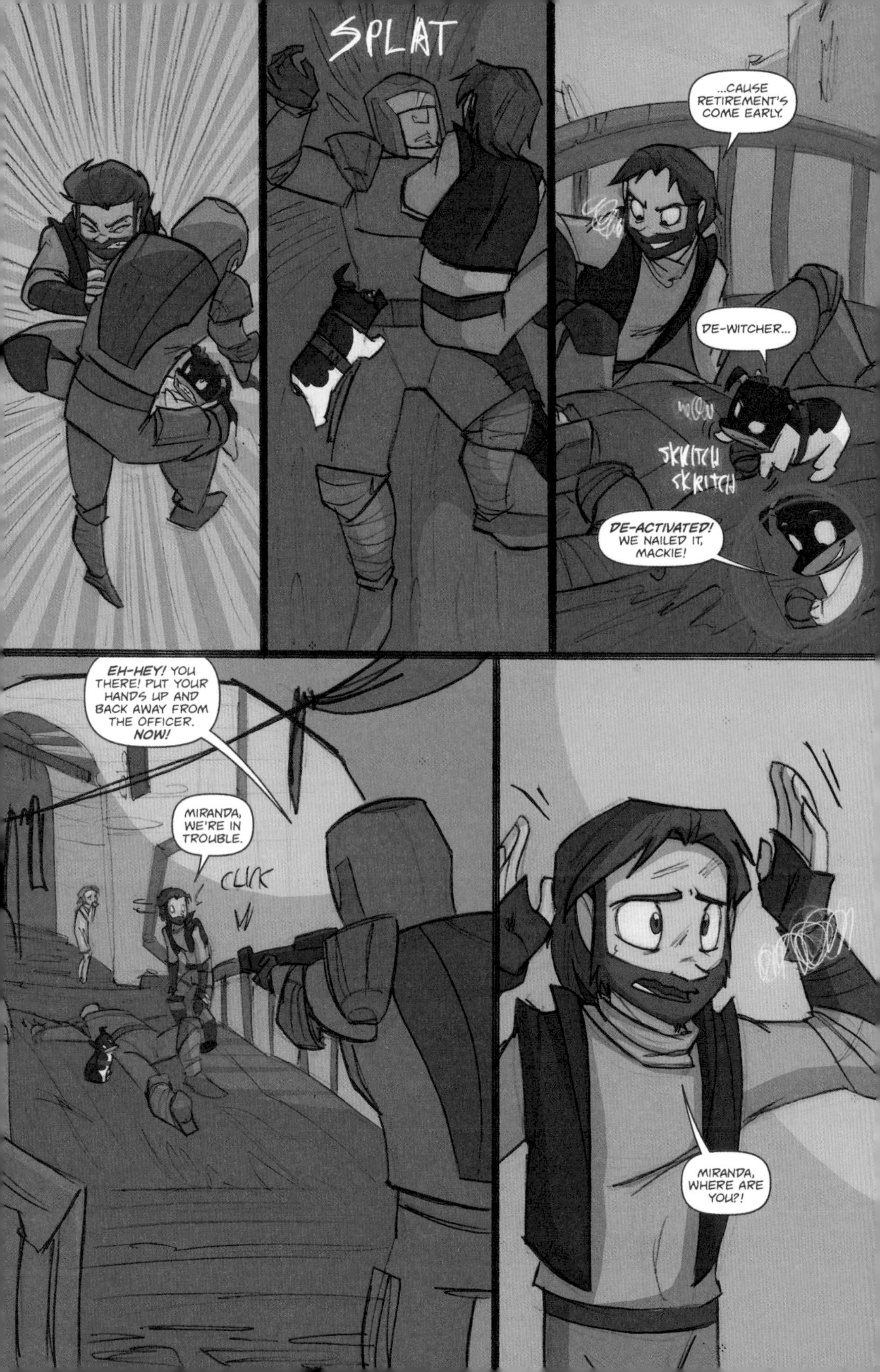
SPLAT
...CAUSE RETIREMENT'S COME EARLY.
DE-WITCHER...
SKRITCH SKRITCH
DE-ACTIVATED! WE NAILED IT, MACKIE!
EH-HEY! YOU THERE! PUT YOUR HANDS UP AND BACK AWAY FROM THE OFFICER. NOW!
MIRANDA, WE'RE IN TROUBLE.
CLICK
MIRANDA, WHERE ARE YOU?!

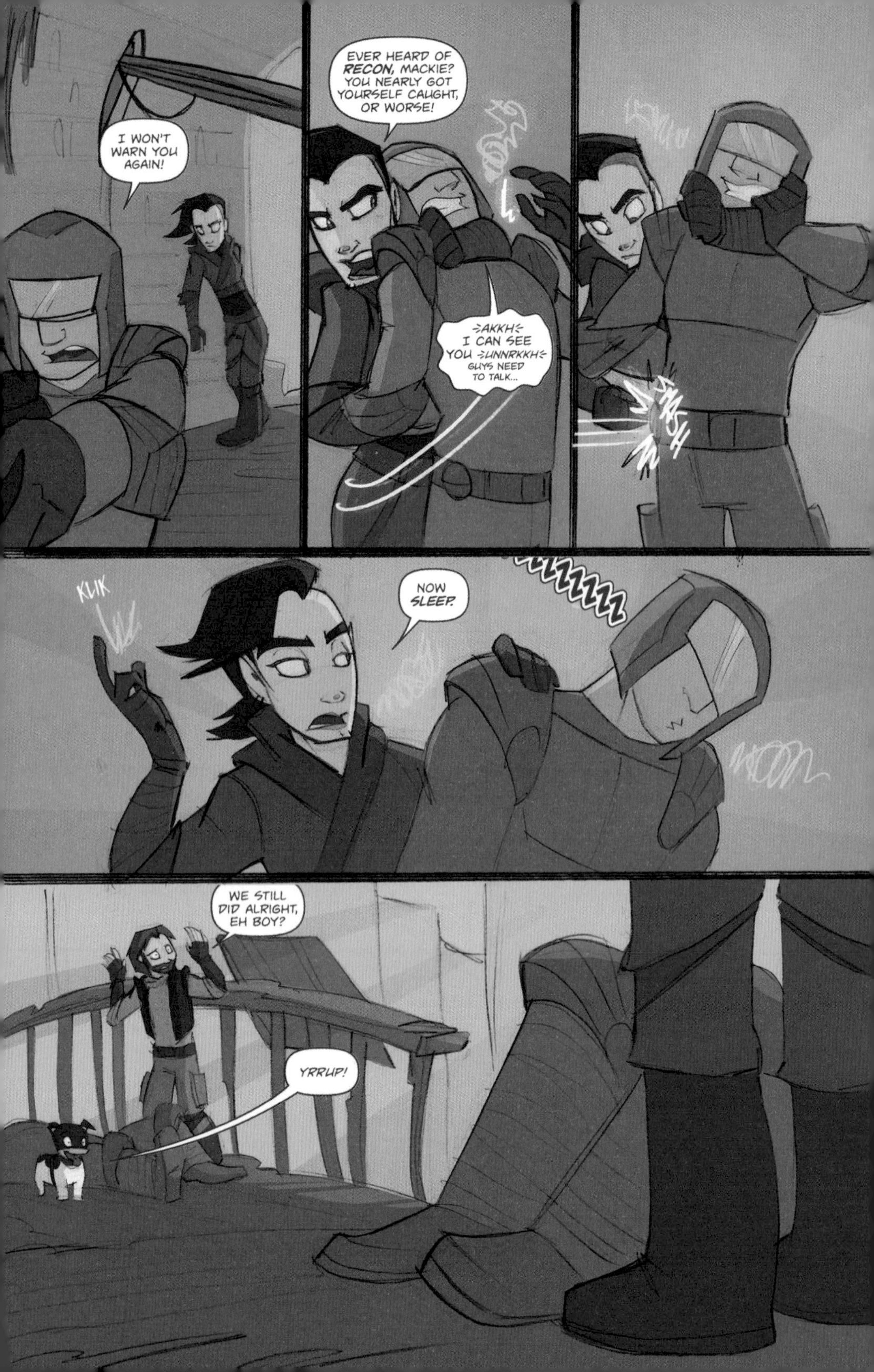

I WON'T WARN YOU AGAIN!
EVER HEARD OF RECON, MACKIE? YOU NEARLY GOT YOURSELF CAUGHT, OR WORSE!
=AKKH= I CAN SEE YOU =UNNRKKH= GUYS NEED TO TALK...
SMASH
KLIK
NOW SLEEP.
ZZZZZZZZ
WE STILL DID ALRIGHT, EH BOY?
YRRUP!

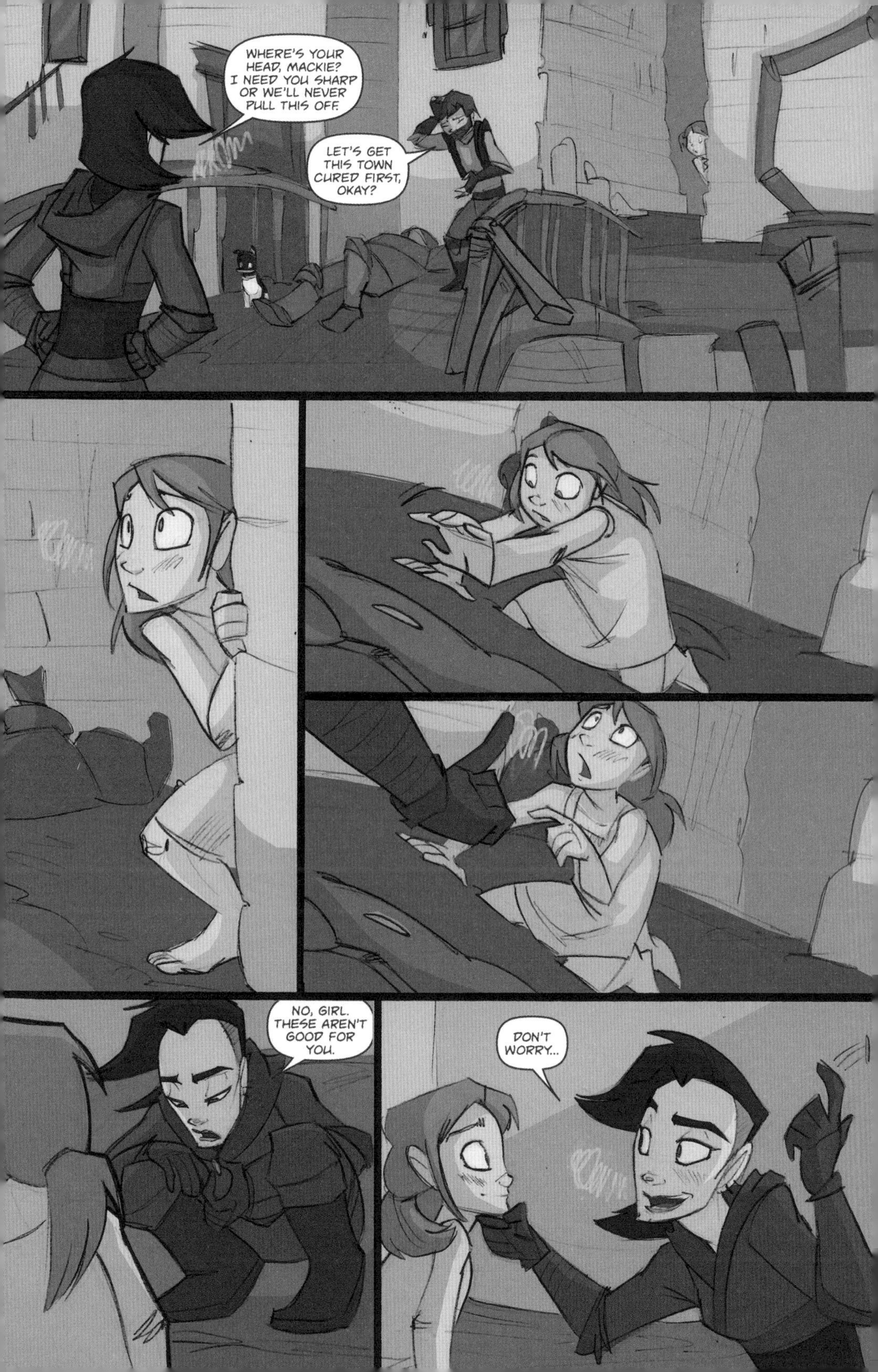
WHERE'S YOUR HEAD, MACKIE? I NEED YOU SHARP OR WE'LL NEVER PULL THIS OFF.
LET'S GET THIS TOWN CURED FIRST, OKAY?
NO, GIRL. THESE AREN'T GOOD FOR YOU.
DON'T WORRY...

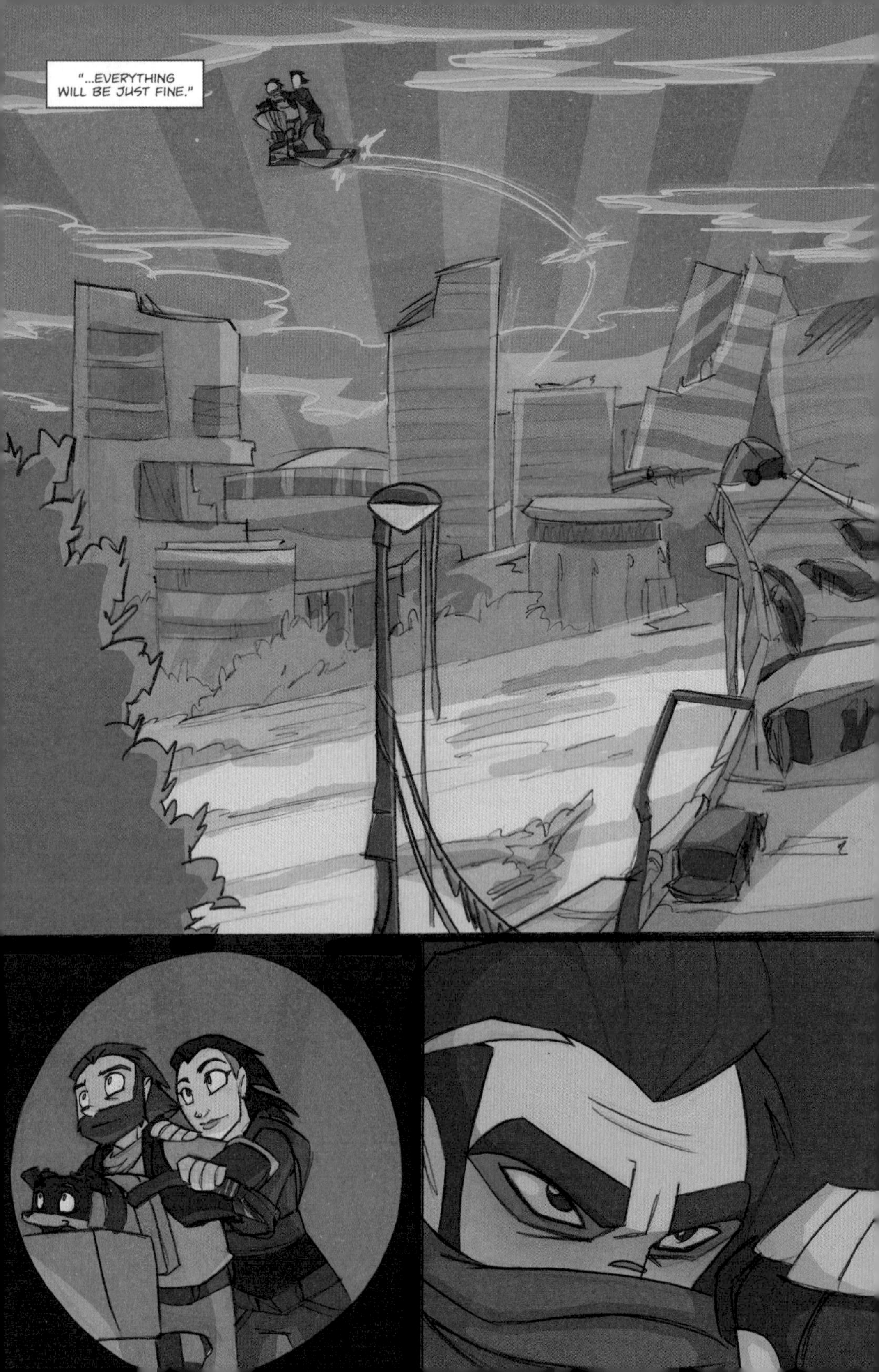
"...EVERYTHING WILL BE JUST FINE."

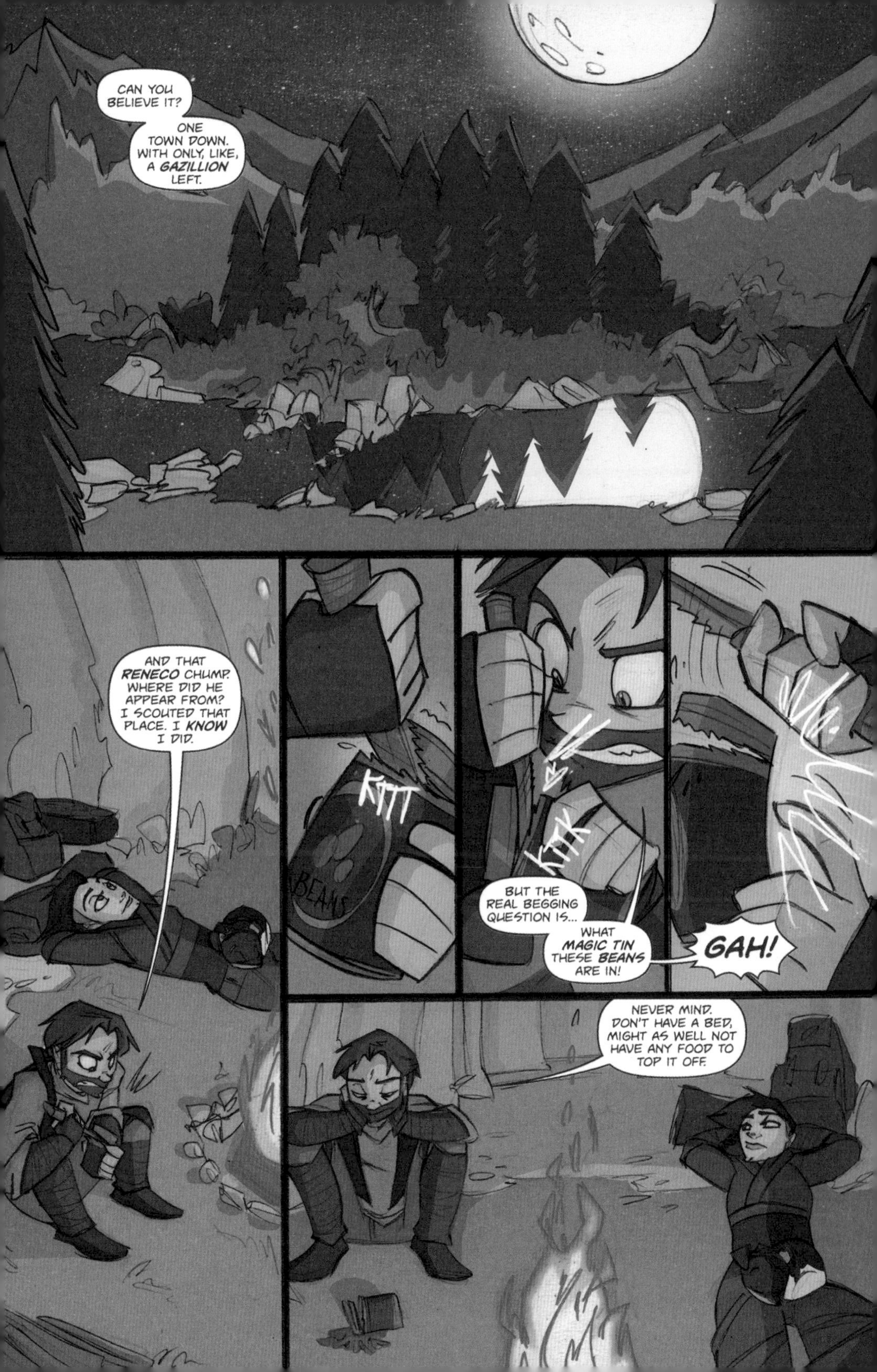
CAN YOU BELIEVE IT?
ONE TOWN DOWN. WITH ONLY, LIKE, A GAZILLION LEFT.
AND THAT RENECO CHUMP. WHERE DID HE APPEAR FROM? I SCOUTED THAT PLACE. I KNOW I DID.
KTTT
BEANS
KTK
BUT THE REAL BEGGING QUESTION IS...
WHAT MAGIC TIN THESE BEANS ARE IN!
GAH!
NEVER MIND. DON'T HAVE A BED, MIGHT AS WELL NOT HAVE ANY FOOD TO TOP IT OFF.

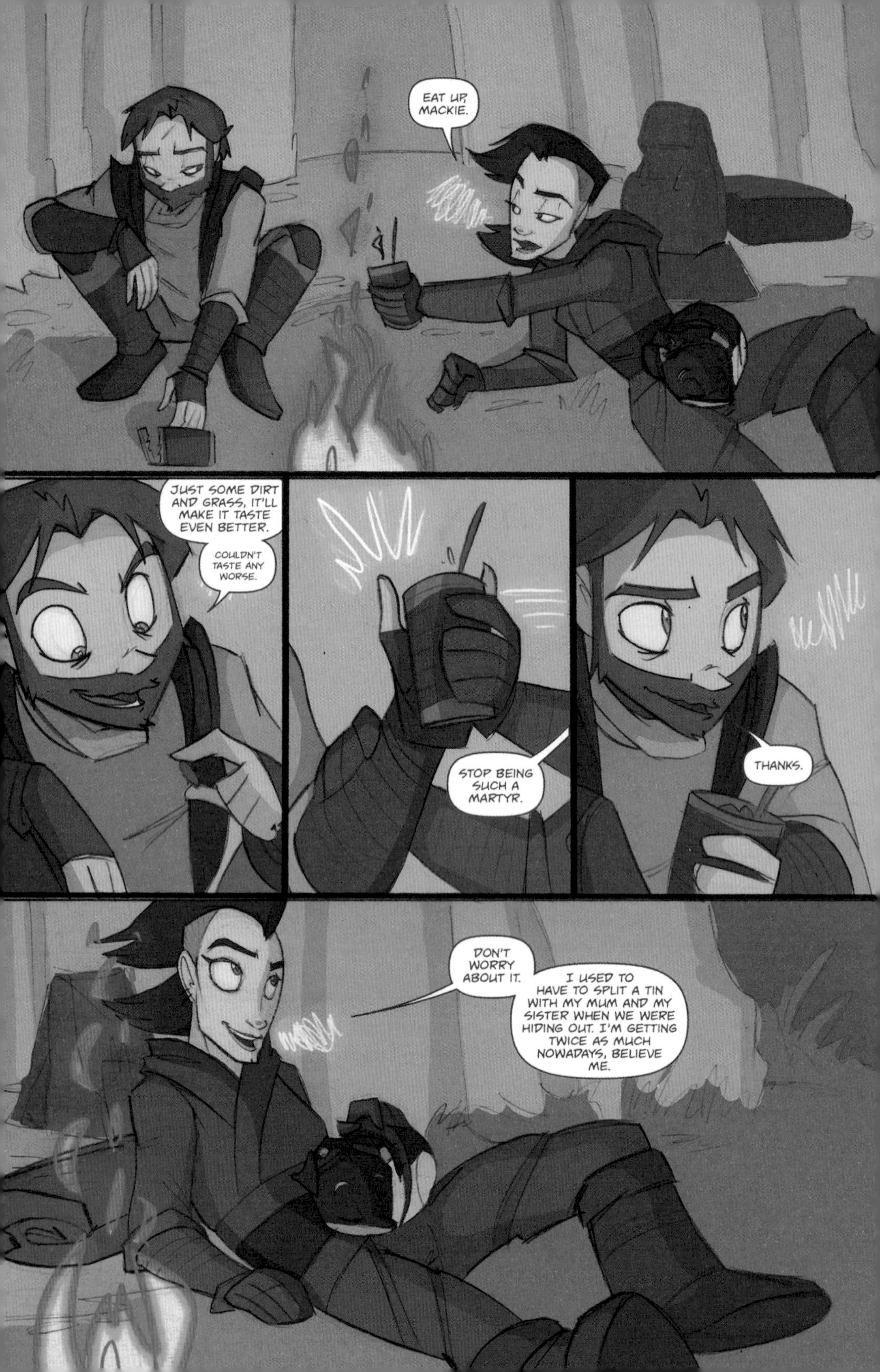
EAT UP, MACKIE.
JUST SOME DIRT AND GRASS, IT'LL MAKE IT TASTE EVEN BETTER.
COULDN'T TASTE ANY WORSE.
STOP BEING SUCH A MARTYR.
THANKS.
DON'T WORRY ABOUT IT.
I USED TO HAVE TO SPLIT A TIN WITH MY MUM AND MY SISTER WHEN WE WERE HIDING OUT. I'M GETTING TWICE AS MUCH NOWADAYS, BELIEVE ME.

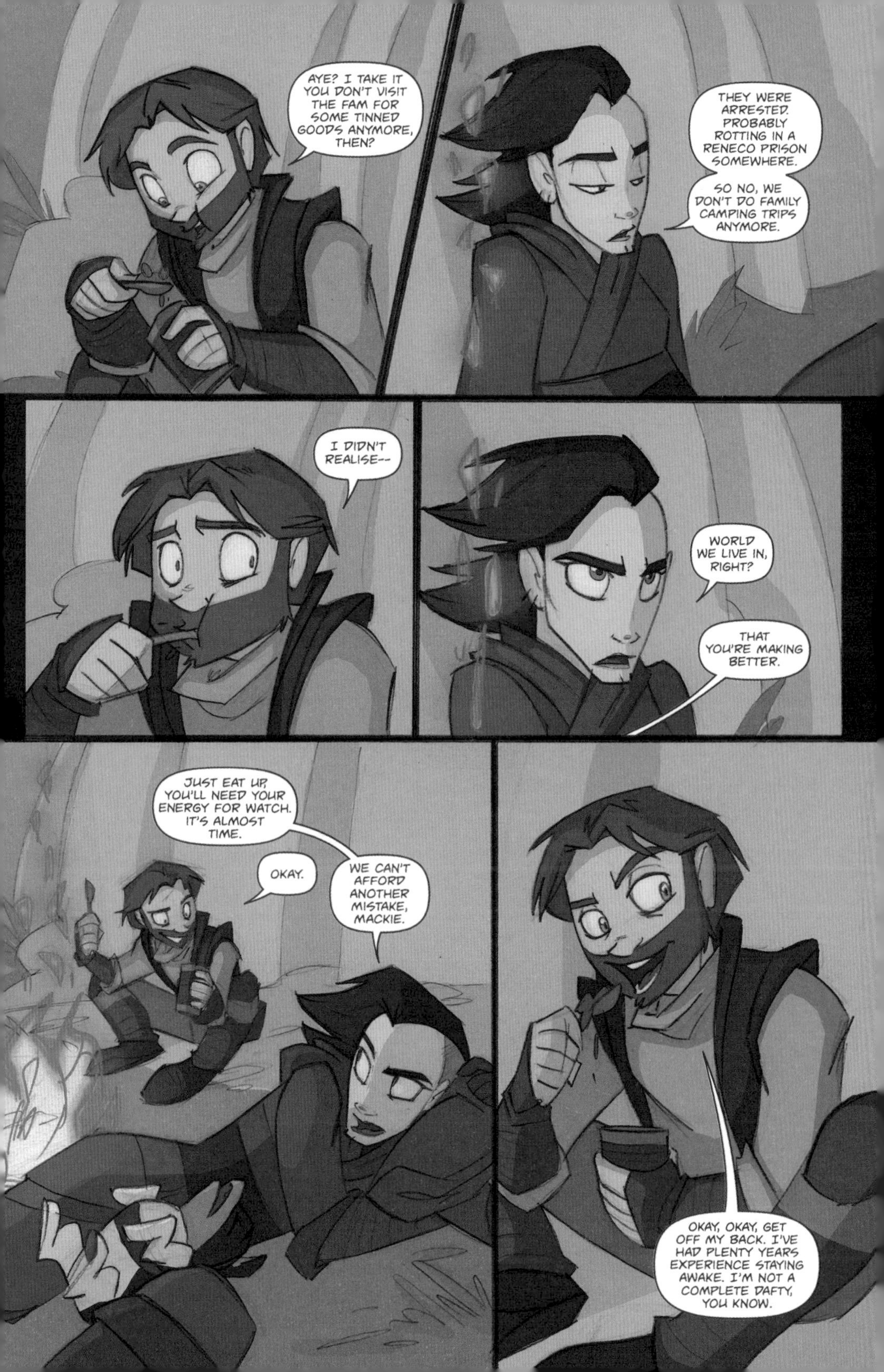
AYE? I TAKE IT YOU DON'T VISIT THE FAM FOR SOME TINNED GOODS ANYMORE, THEN?
THEY WERE ARRESTED. PROBABLY ROTTING IN A RENECO PRISON SOMEWHERE.
SO NO, WE DON'T DO FAMILY CAMPING TRIPS ANYMORE.
I DIDN'T REALISE--
WORLD WE LIVE IN, RIGHT?
THAT YOU'RE MAKING BETTER.
JUST EAT UP. YOU'LL NEED YOUR ENERGY FOR WATCH. IT'S ALMOST TIME.
OKAY.
WE CAN'T AFFORD ANOTHER MISTAKE, MACKIE.
OKAY, OKAY, GET OFF MY BACK. I'VE HAD PLENTY YEARS EXPERIENCE STAYING AWAKE. I'M NOT A COMPLETE DAFTY, YOU KNOW.

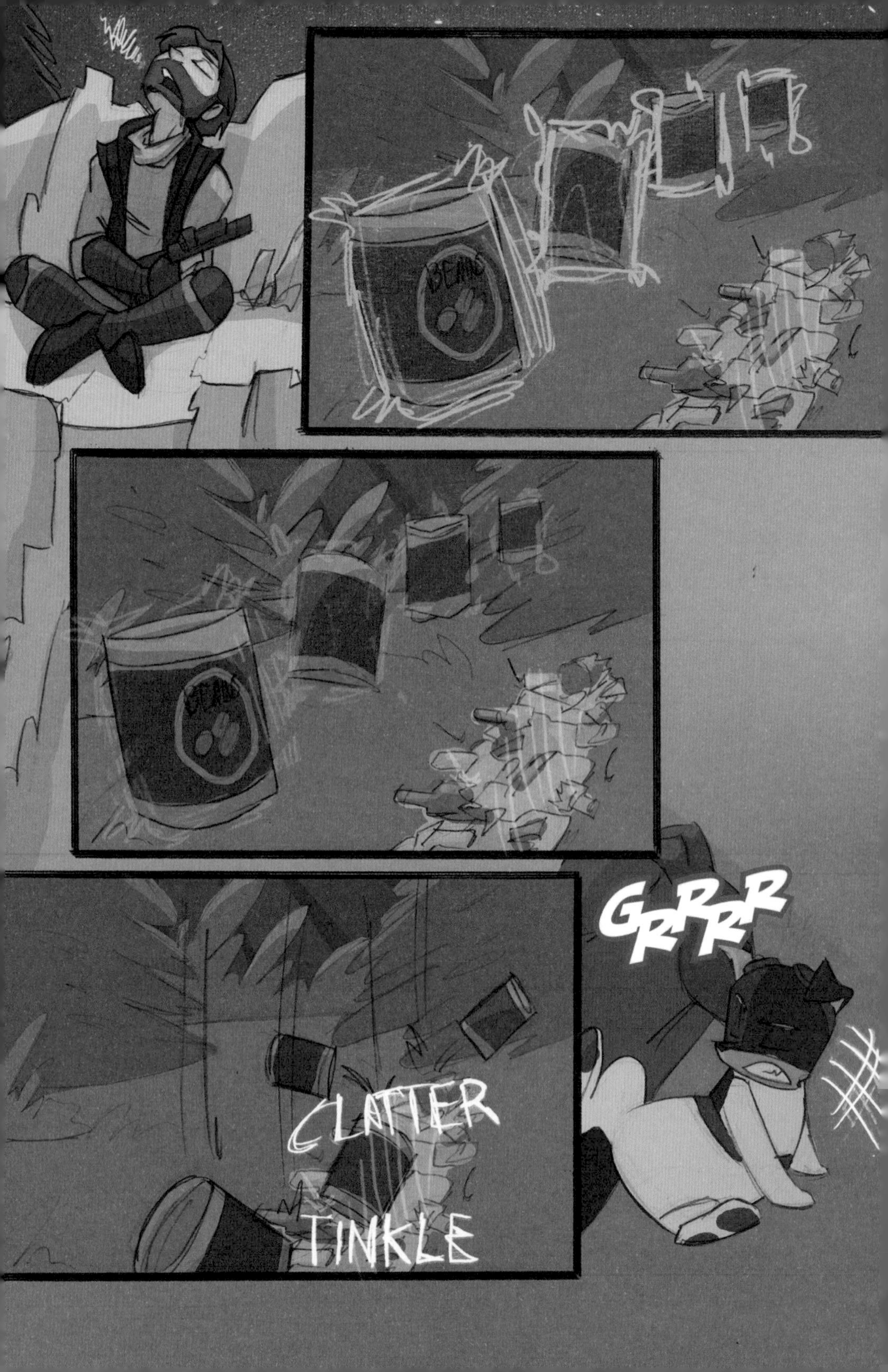
GRRRR
CLATTER
TINKLE

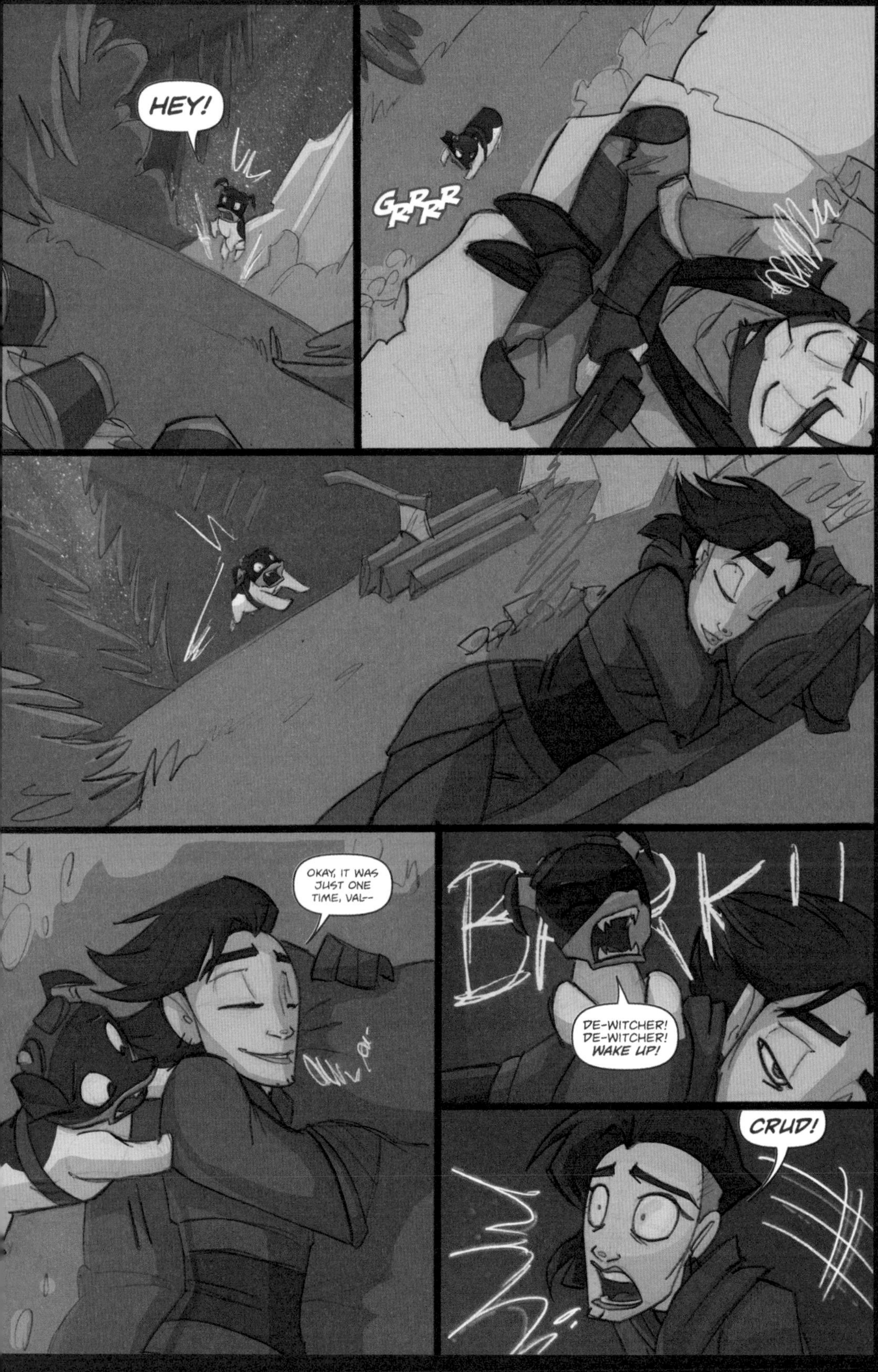
HEY!
GRRRR
OKAY, IT WAS JUST ONE TIME, VAL--
DE-WITCHER! DE-WITCHER! WAKE UP!
CRUD!

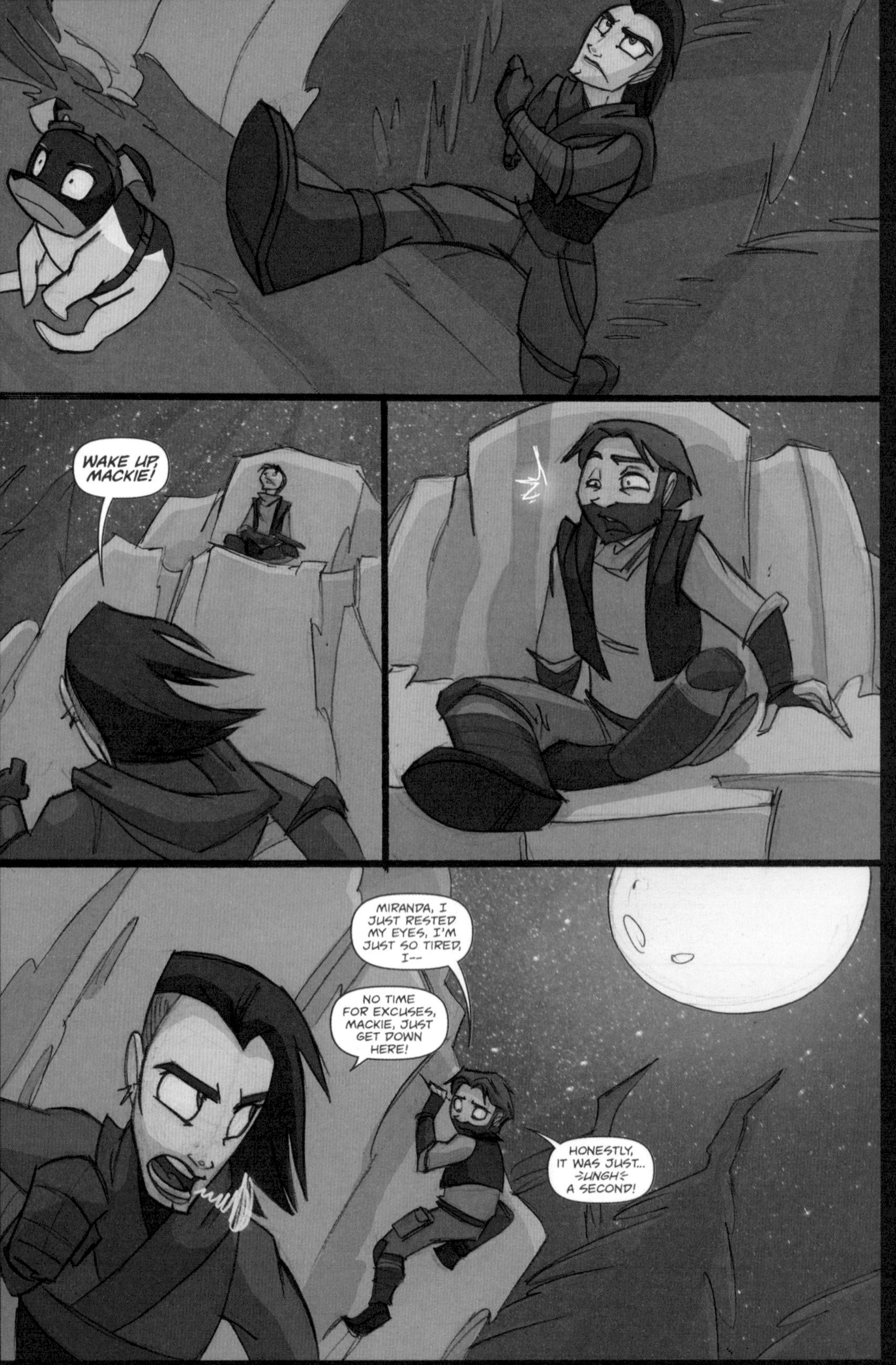
WAKE UP, MACKIE!
MIRANDA, I JUST RESTED MY EYES, I'M JUST SO TIRED, I--
NO TIME FOR EXCUSES, MACKIE, JUST GET DOWN HERE!
HONESTLY, IT WAS JUST... UNGH A SECOND!

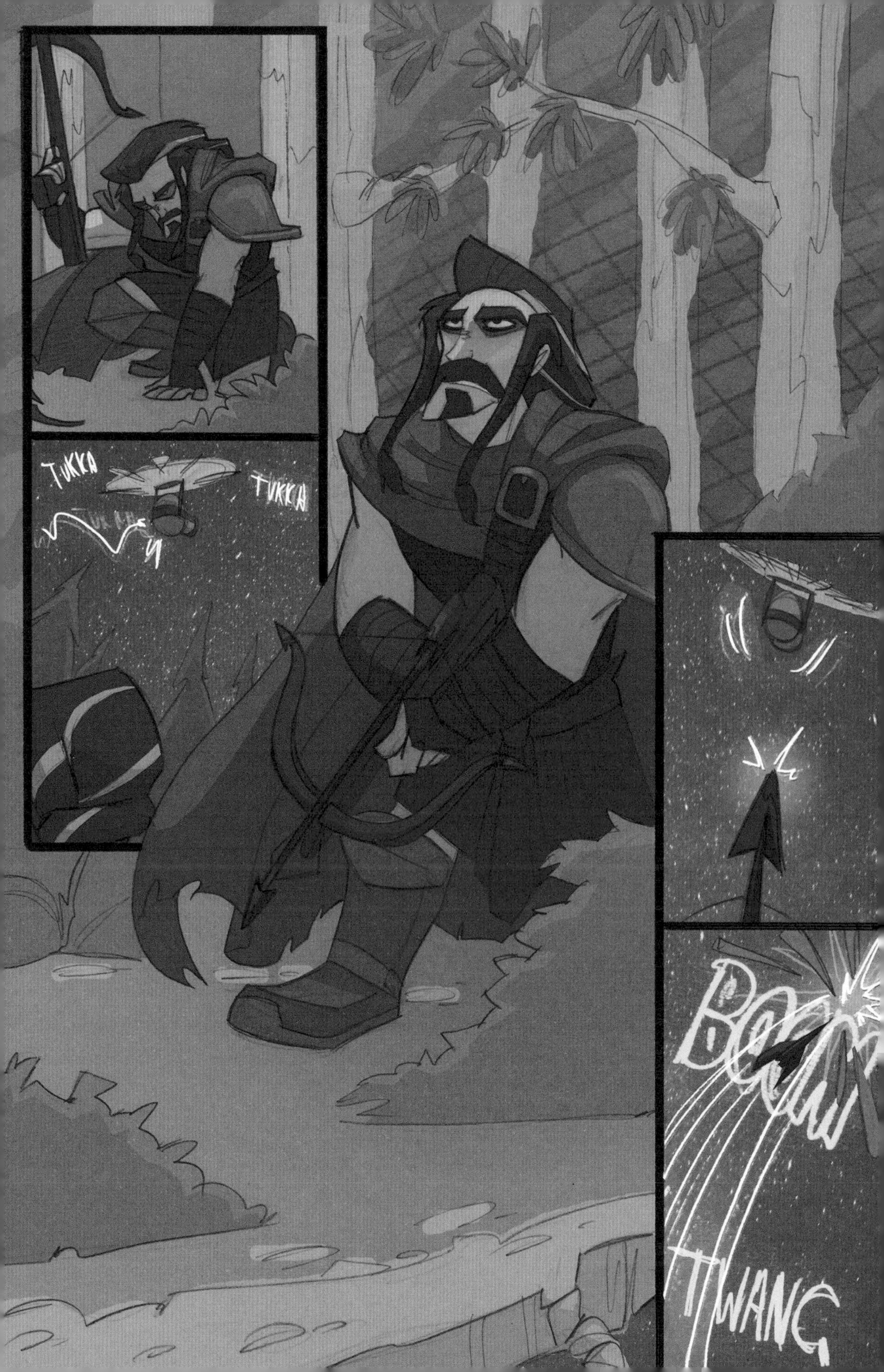
TUKKA
TUKKA
TWANG

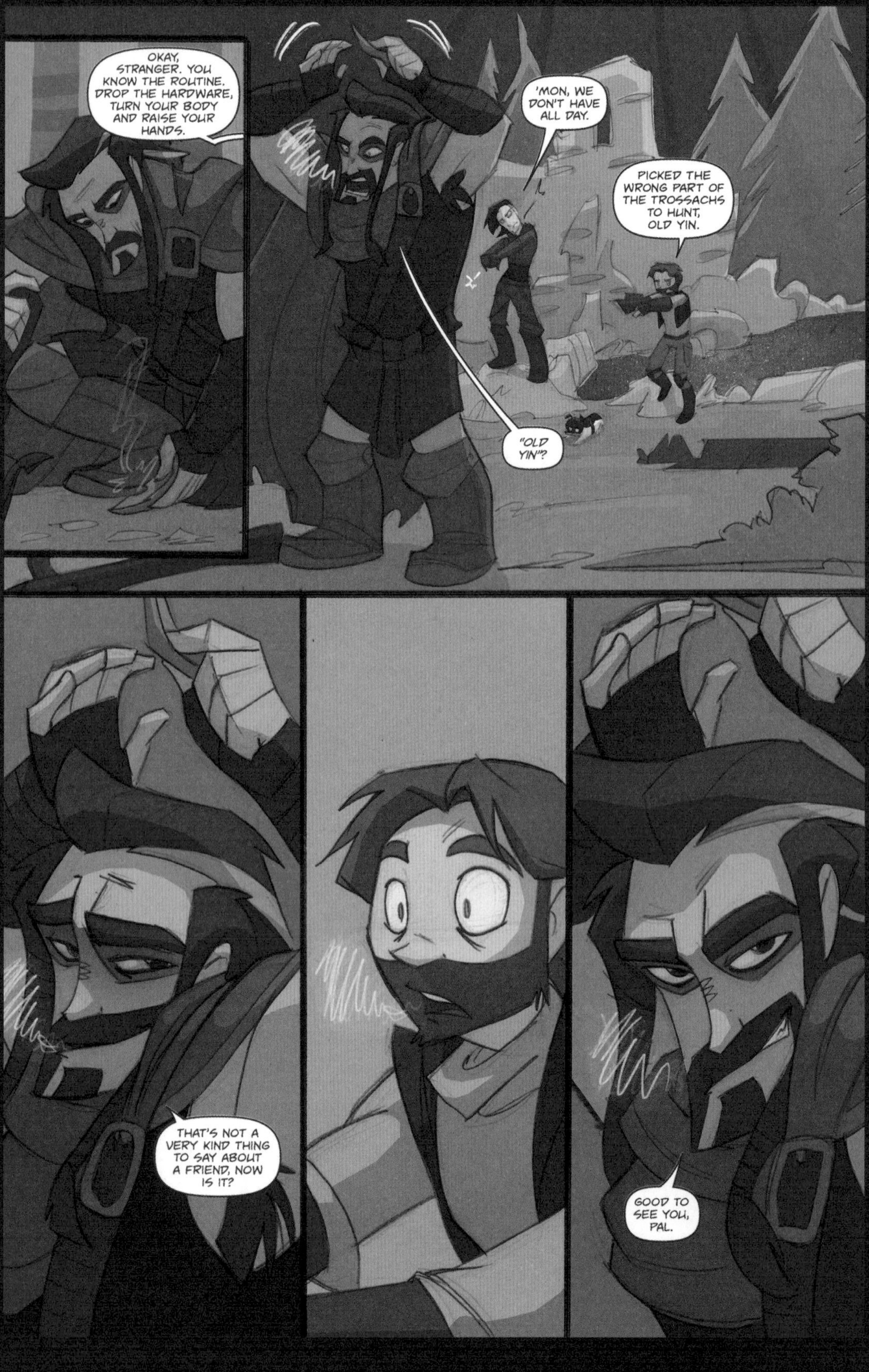
OKAY, STRANGER. YOU KNOW THE ROUTINE. DROP THE HARDWARE, TURN YOUR BODY AND RAISE YOUR HANDS.
'MON, WE DON'T HAVE ALL DAY.
PICKED THE WRONG PART OF THE TROSSACHS TO HUNT, OLD YIN.
"OLD YIN"?
THAT'S NOT A VERY KIND THING TO SAY ABOUT A FRIEND, NOW IS IT?
GOOD TO SEE YOU, PAL.

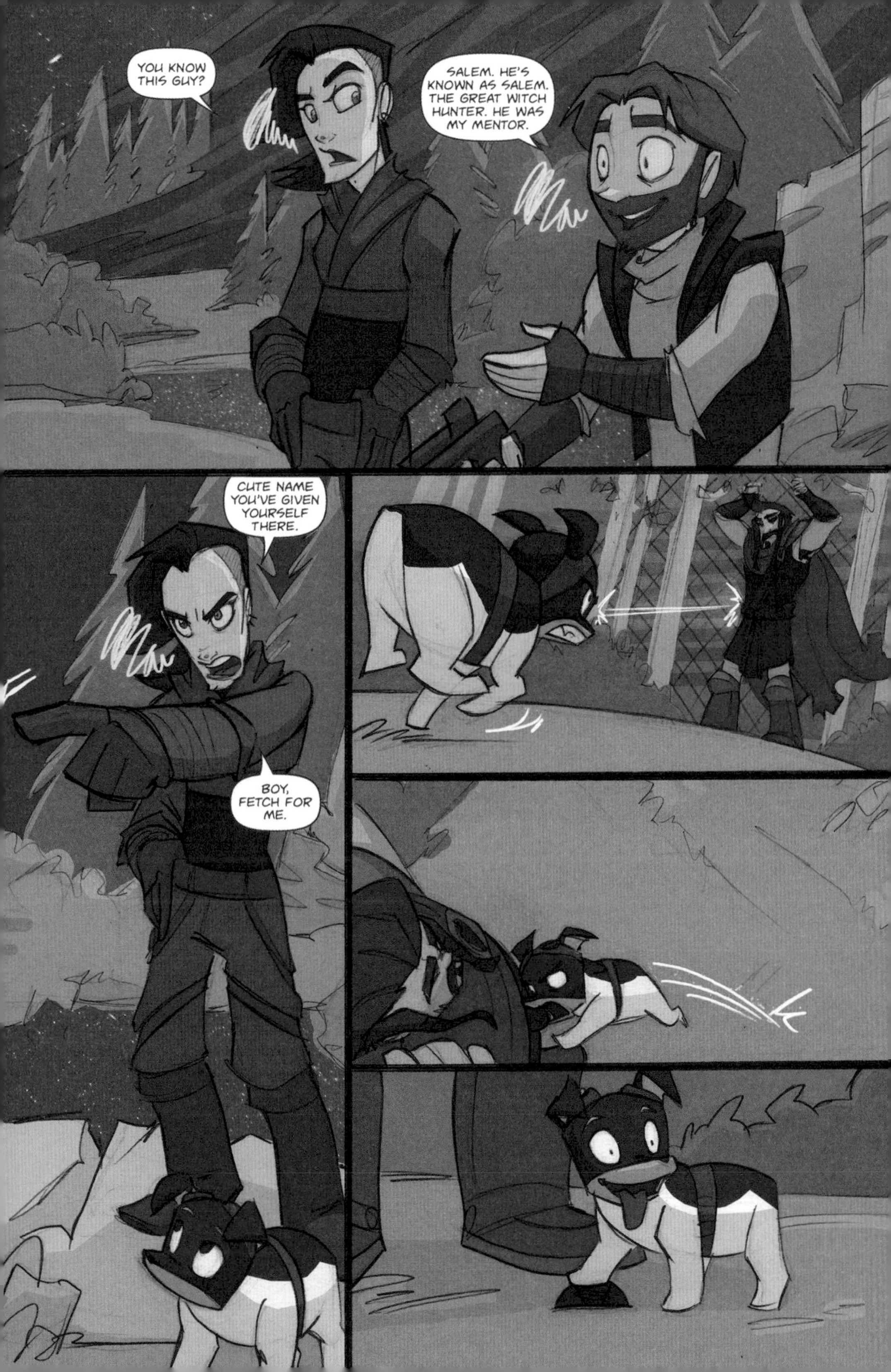
YOU KNOW THIS GUY?
SALEM. HE'S KNOWN AS SALEM. THE GREAT WITCH HUNTER. HE WAS MY MENTOR.
CUTE NAME YOU'VE GIVEN YOURSELF THERE.
BOY, FETCH FOR ME.

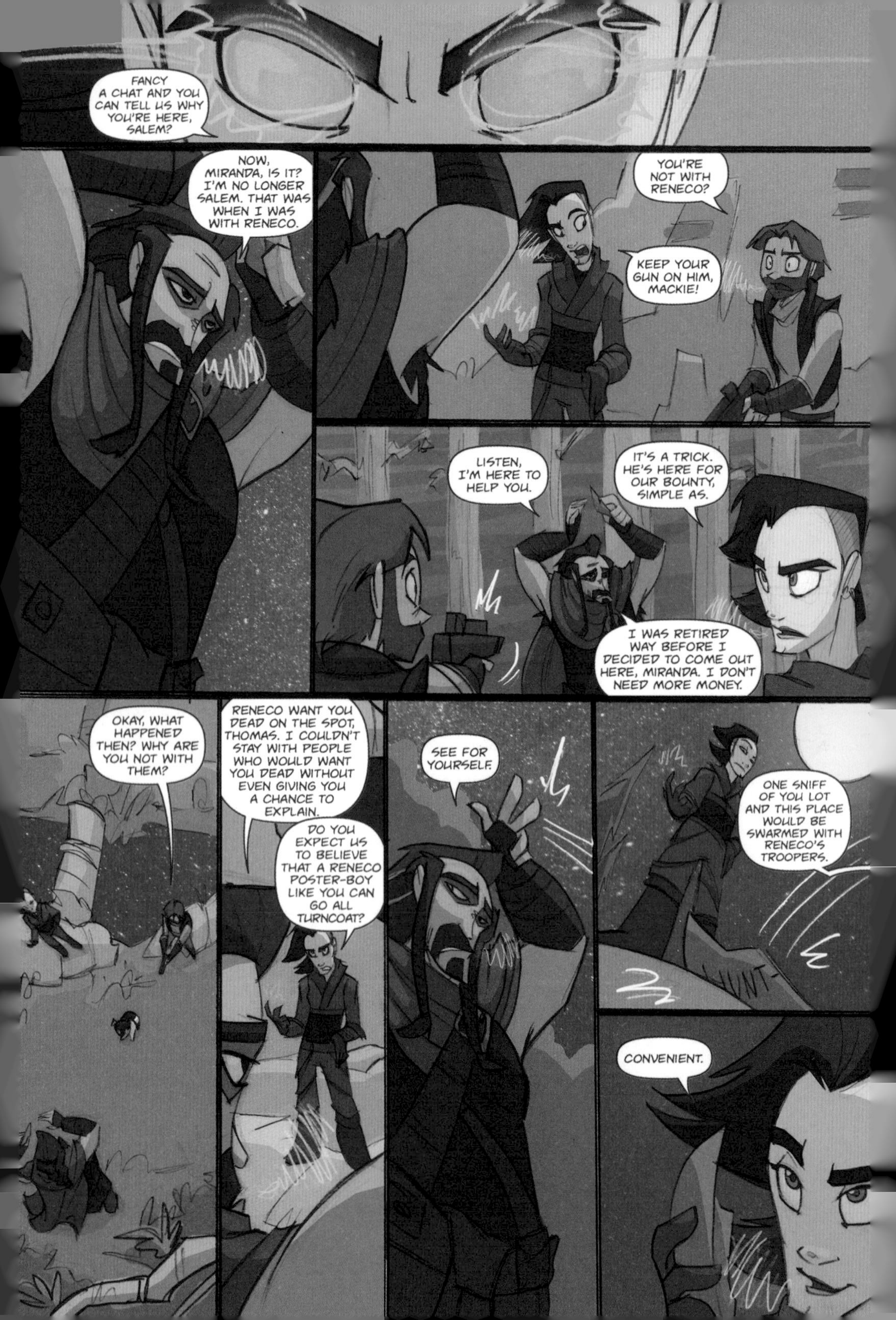
FANCY A CHAT AND YOU CAN TELL US WHY YOU'RE HERE, SALEM?
NOW, MIRANDA, IS IT? I'M NO LONGER SALEM. THAT WAS WHEN I WAS WITH RENECO.
YOU'RE NOT WITH RENECO?
KEEP YOUR GUN ON HIM, MACKIE!
LISTEN, I'M HERE TO HELP YOU.
IT'S A TRICK. HE'S HERE FOR OUR BOUNTY, SIMPLE AS.
I WAS RETIRED WAY BEFORE I DECIDED TO COME OUT HERE, MIRANDA. I DON'T NEED MORE MONEY.
OKAY, WHAT HAPPENED THEN? WHY ARE YOU NOT WITH THEM?
RENECO WANT YOU DEAD ON THE SPOT, THOMAS. I COULDN'T STAY WITH PEOPLE WHO WOULD WANT YOU DEAD WITHOUT EVEN GIVING YOU A CHANCE TO EXPLAIN.
DO YOU EXPECT US TO BELIEVE THAT A RENECO POSTER-BOY LIKE YOU CAN GO ALL TURNCOAT?
SEE FOR YOURSELF.
ONE SNIFF OF YOU LOT AND THIS PLACE WOULD BE SWARMED WITH RENECO'S TROOPERS.
HUNT-
CONVENIENT.

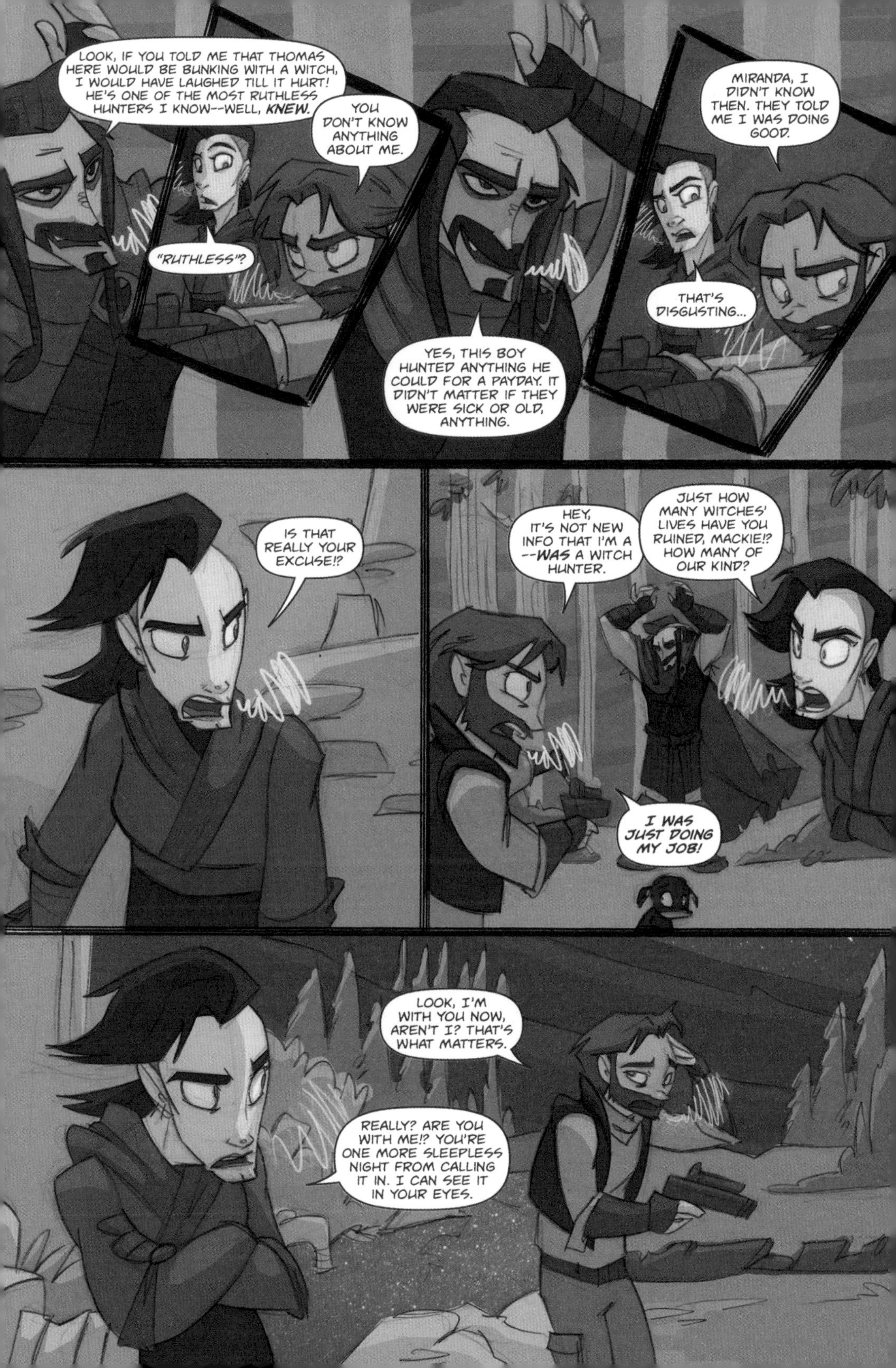
LOOK, IF YOU TOLD ME THAT THOMAS HERE WOULD BE BUNKING WITH A WITCH, I WOULD HAVE LAUGHED TILL IT HURT! HE'S ONE OF THE MOST RUTHLESS HUNTERS I KNOW--WELL, KNEW.
YOU DON'T KNOW ANYTHING ABOUT ME.
"RUTHLESS"?
YES, THIS BOY HUNTED ANYTHING HE COULD FOR A PAYDAY. IT DIDN'T MATTER IF THEY WERE SICK OR OLD, ANYTHING.
MIRANDA, I DIDN'T KNOW THEN. THEY TOLD ME I WAS DOING GOOD.
THAT'S DISGUSTING...
IS THAT REALLY YOUR EXCUSE!?
HEY, IT'S NOT NEW INFO THAT I'M A --WAS A WITCH HUNTER.
JUST HOW MANY WITCHES' LIVES HAVE YOU RUINED, MACKIE!? HOW MANY OF OUR KIND?
I WAS JUST DOING MY JOB!
LOOK, I'M WITH YOU NOW, AREN'T I? THAT'S WHAT MATTERS.
REALLY? ARE YOU WITH ME!? YOU'RE ONE MORE SLEEPLESS NIGHT FROM CALLING IT IN. I CAN SEE IT IN YOUR EYES.

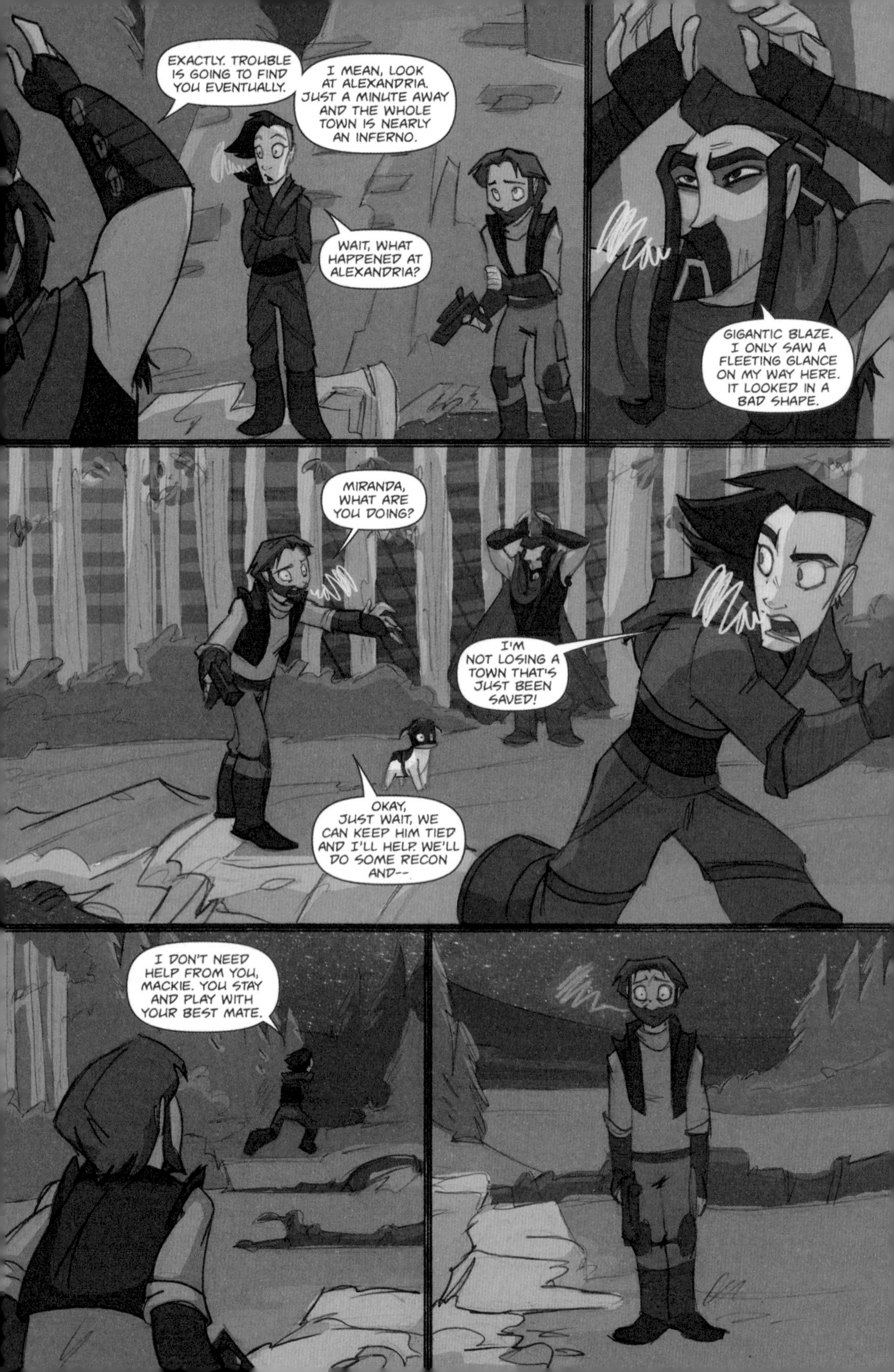
EXACTLY. TROUBLE IS GOING TO FIND YOU EVENTUALLY.
I MEAN, LOOK AT ALEXANDRIA. JUST A MINUTE AWAY AND THE WHOLE TOWN IS NEARLY AN INFERNO.
WAIT, WHAT HAPPENED AT ALEXANDRIA?
GIGANTIC BLAZE. I ONLY SAW A FLEETING GLANCE ON MY WAY HERE. IT LOOKED IN A BAD SHAPE.
MIRANDA, WHAT ARE YOU DOING?
I'M NOT LOSING A TOWN THAT'S JUST BEEN SAVED!
OKAY, JUST WAIT, WE CAN KEEP HIM TIED AND I'LL HELP. WE'LL DO SOME RECON AND--.
I DON'T NEED HELP FROM YOU, MACKIE. YOU STAY AND PLAY WITH YOUR BEST MATE.

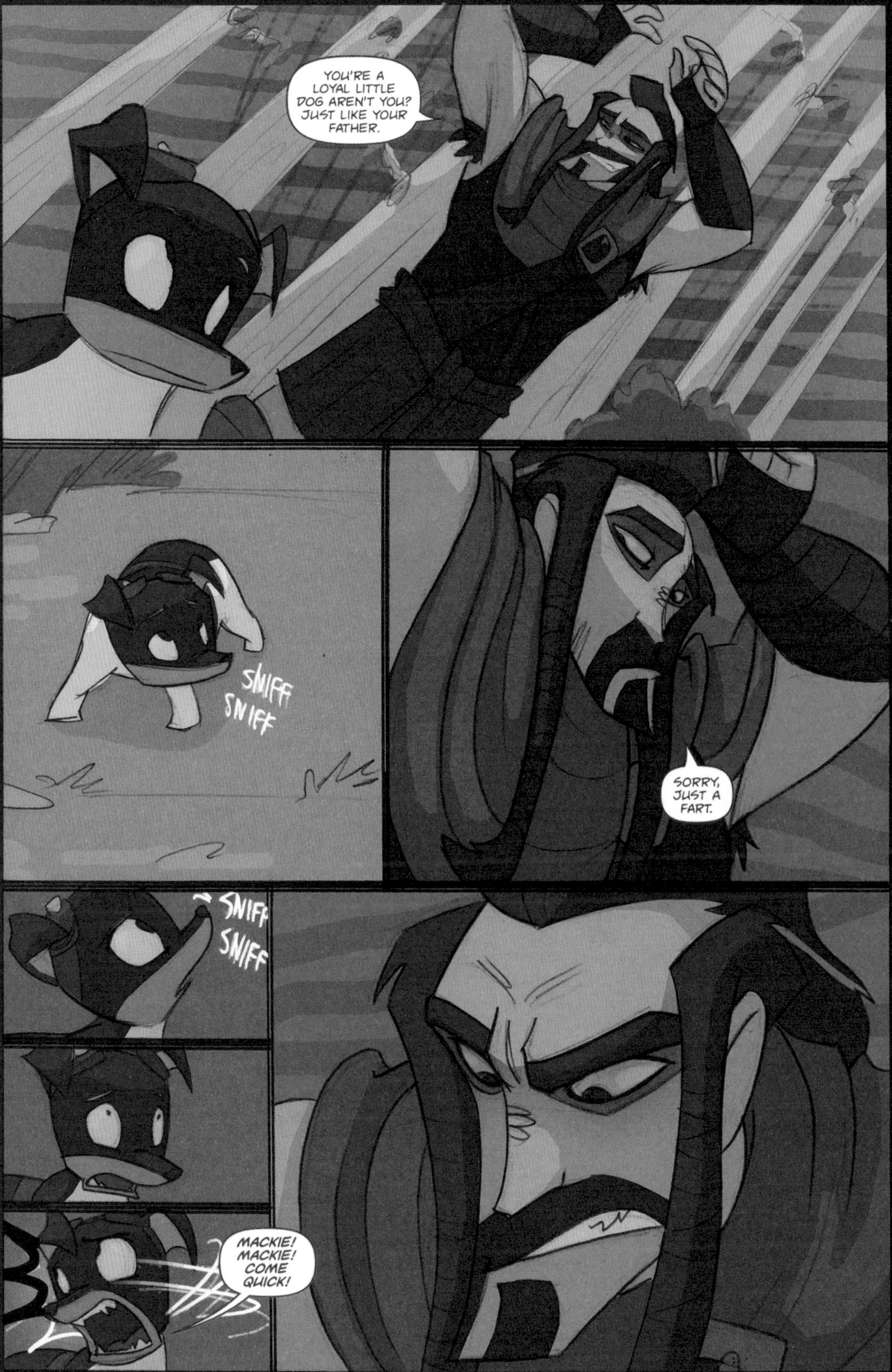
YOU'RE A LOYAL LITTLE DOG AREN'T YOU? JUST LIKE YOUR FATHER.
SNIFF SNIFF
SORRY, JUST A FART.
SNIFF SNIFF
MACKIE! MACKIE! COME QUICK!

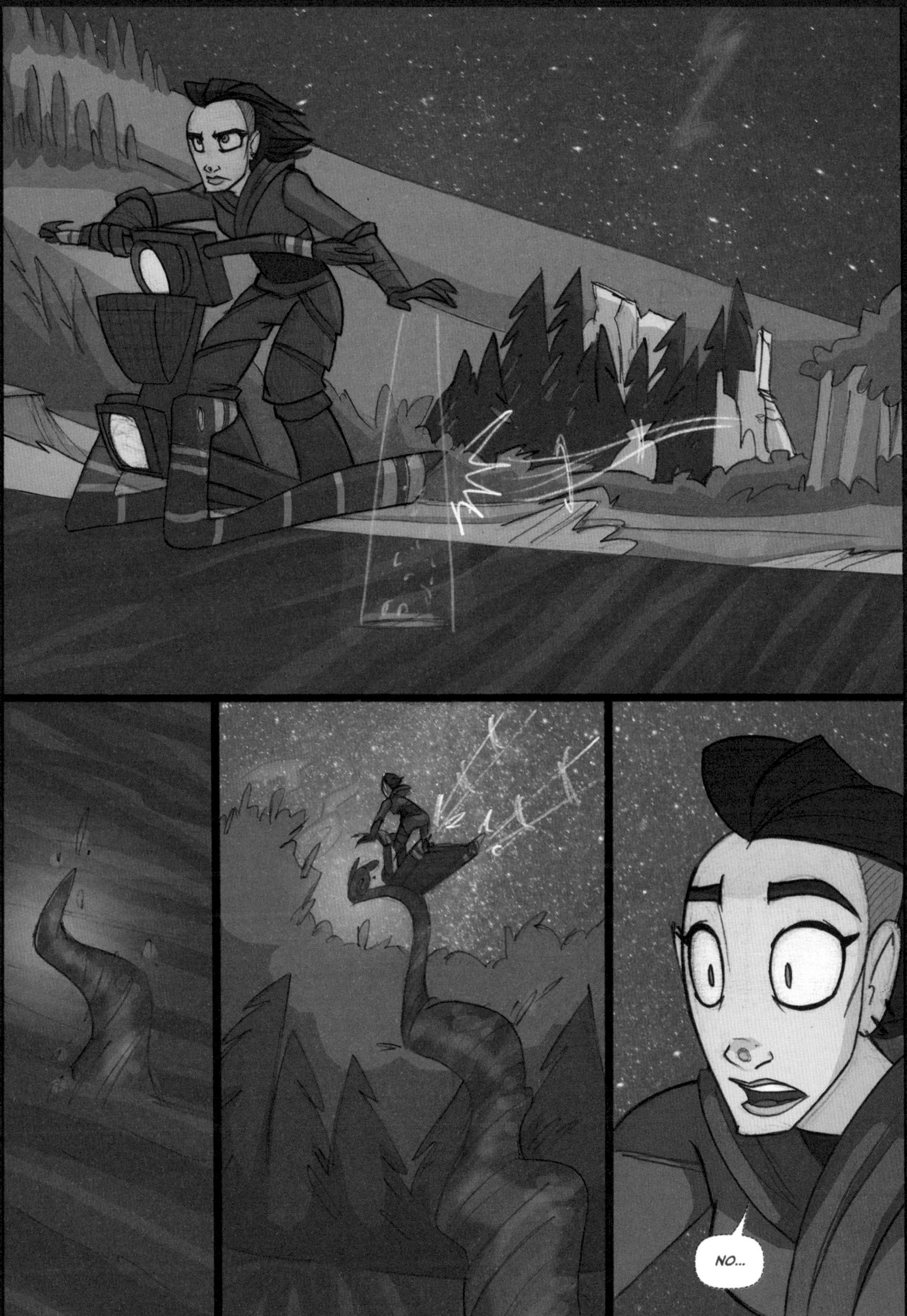
NO...

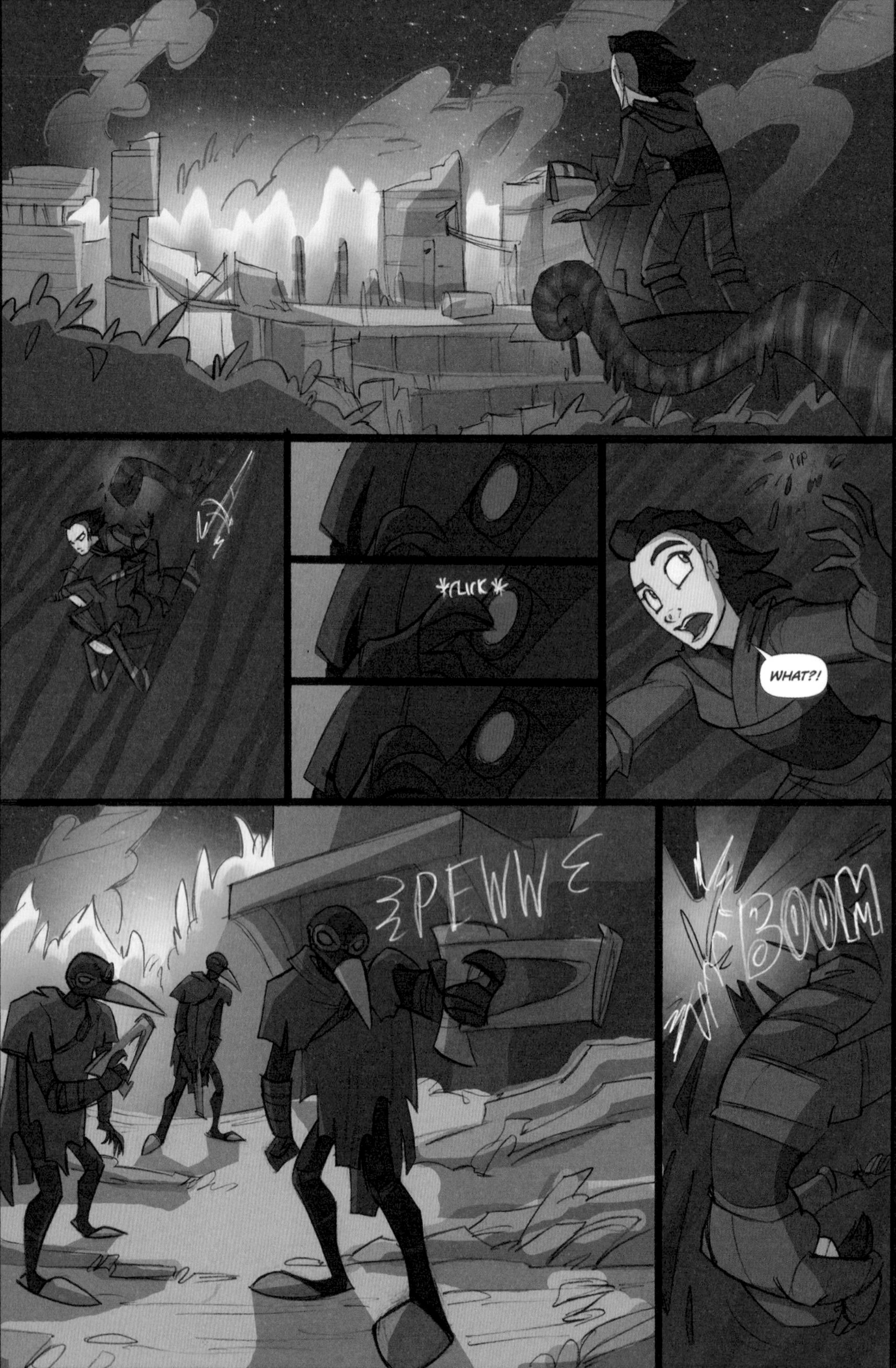
click
WHAT?!
PEWW
BOOM

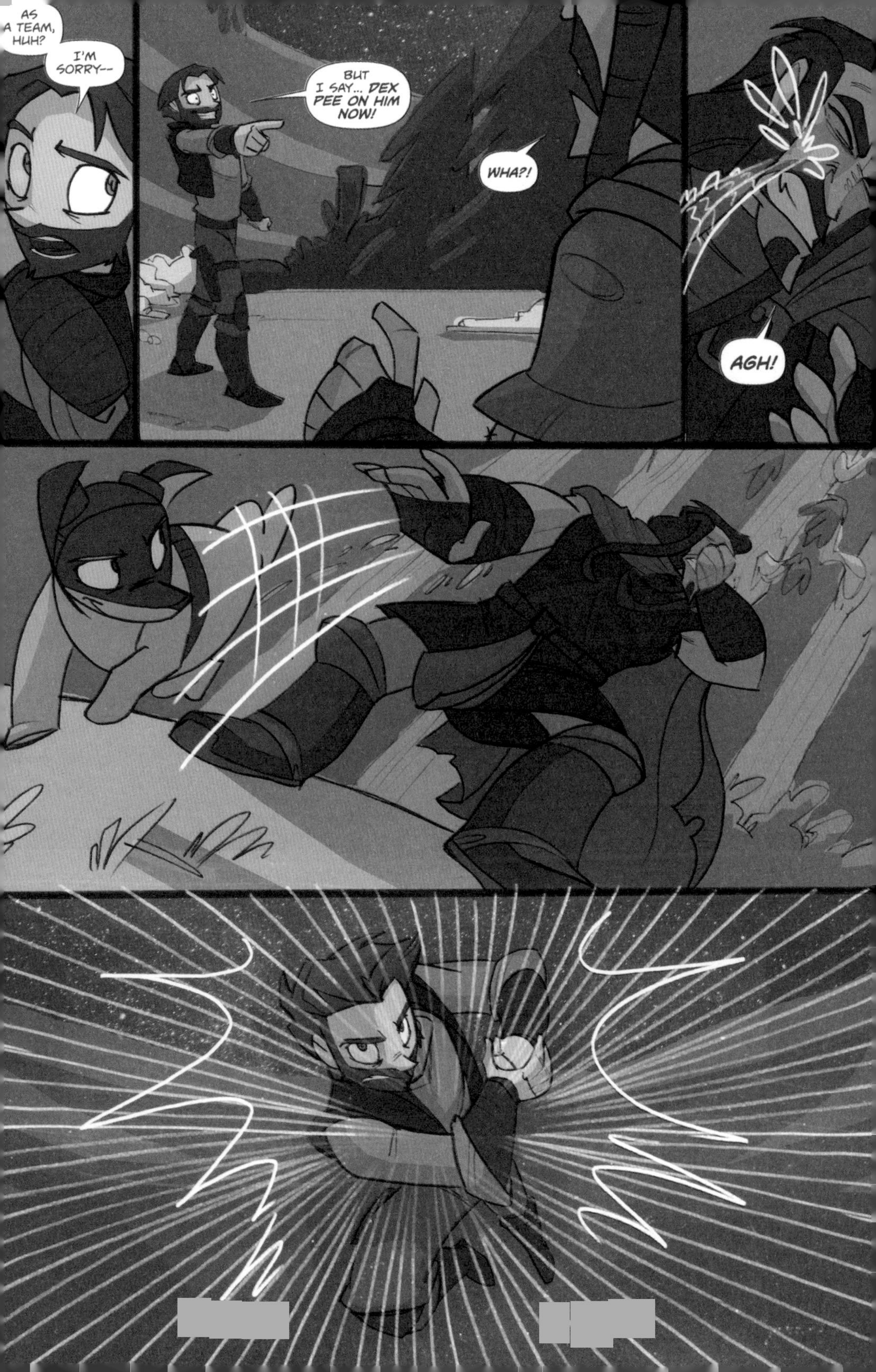
AS A TEAM, HUH?
I'M SORRY--
BUT I SAY... DEX PEE ON HIM NOW!
WHA?!
AGH!

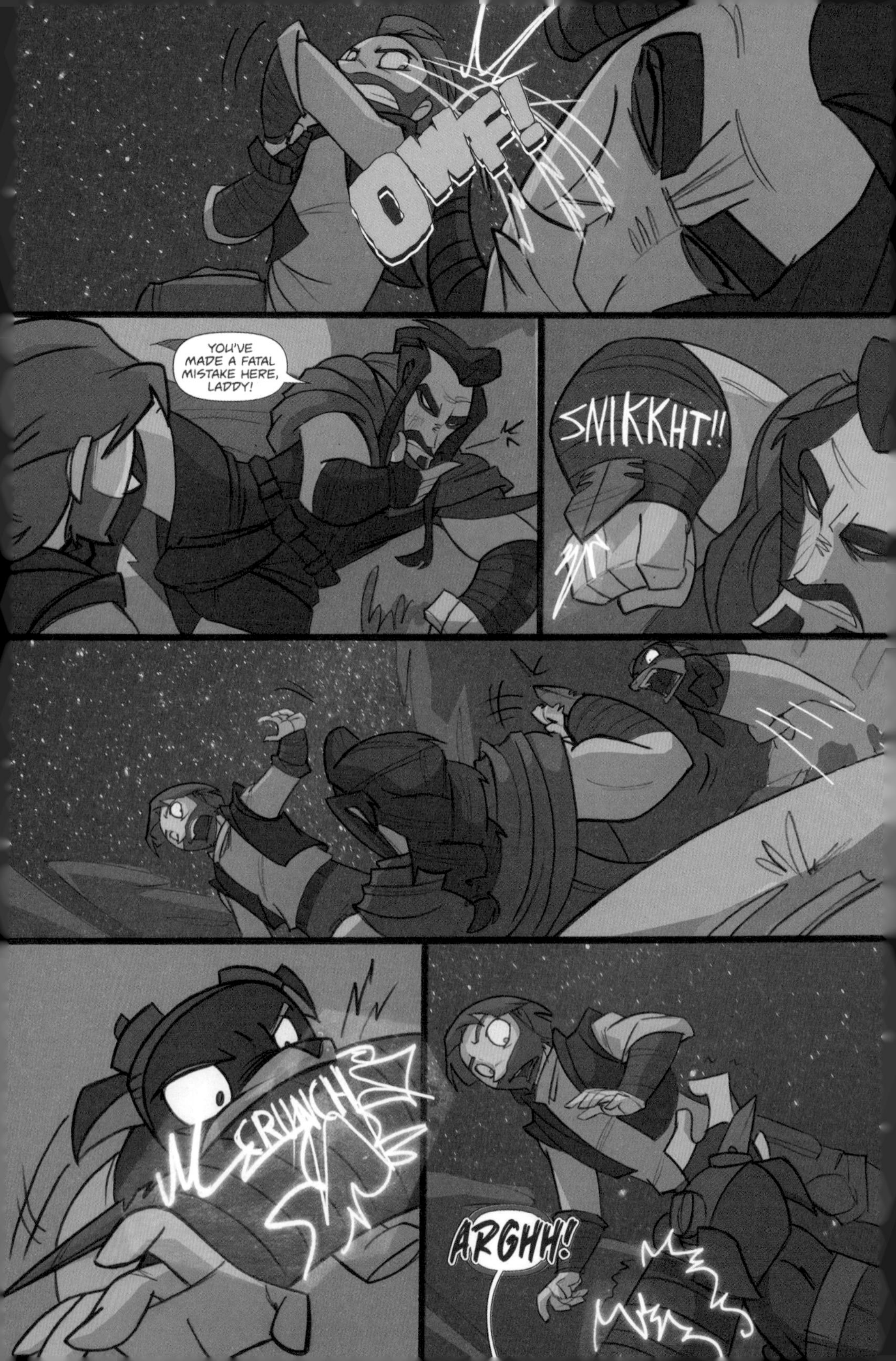
OOMF!
YOU'VE MADE A FATAL MISTAKE HERE, LADDY!
SNIKKHT!!
CRUNCH
ARGHH!

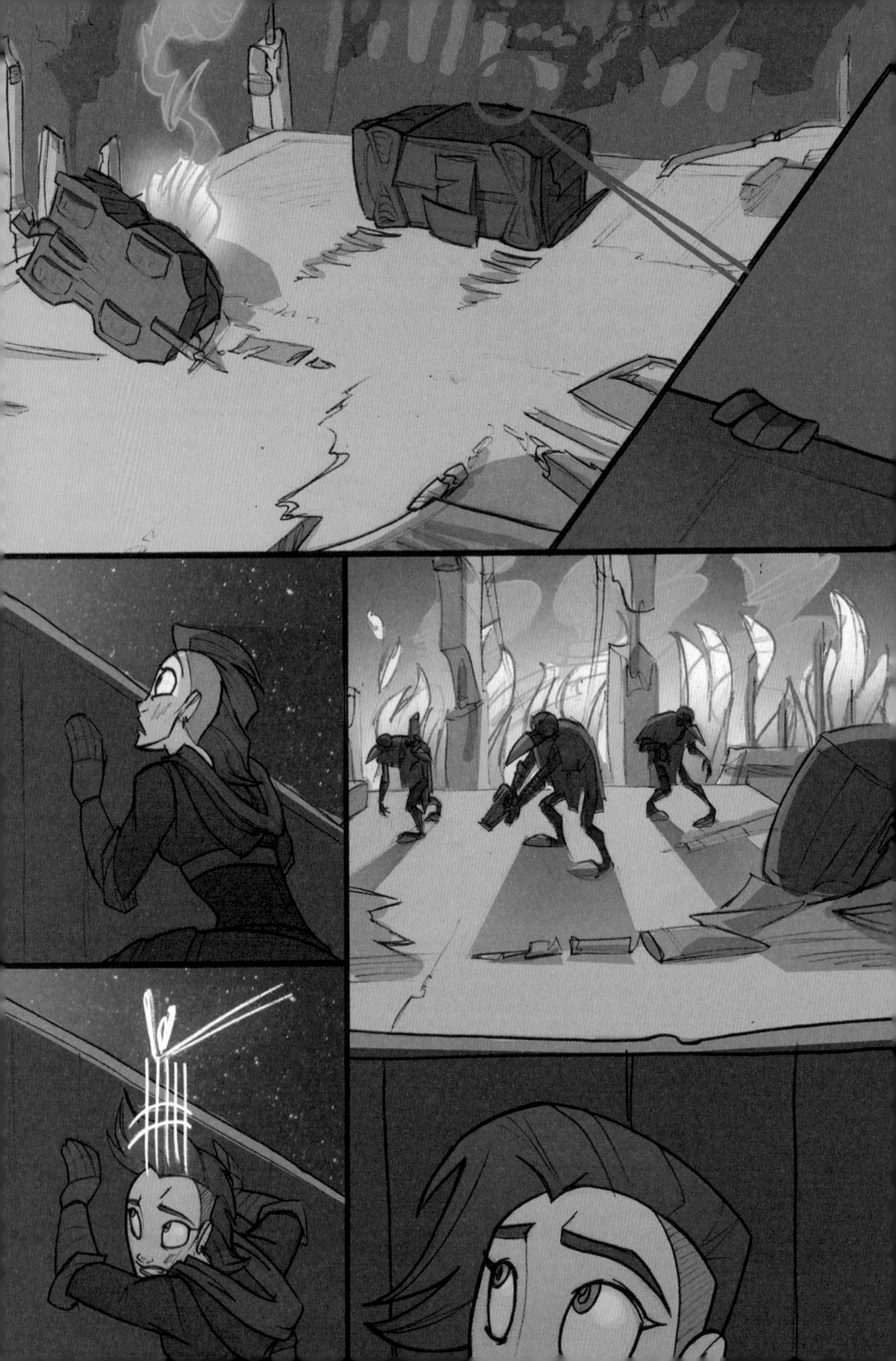

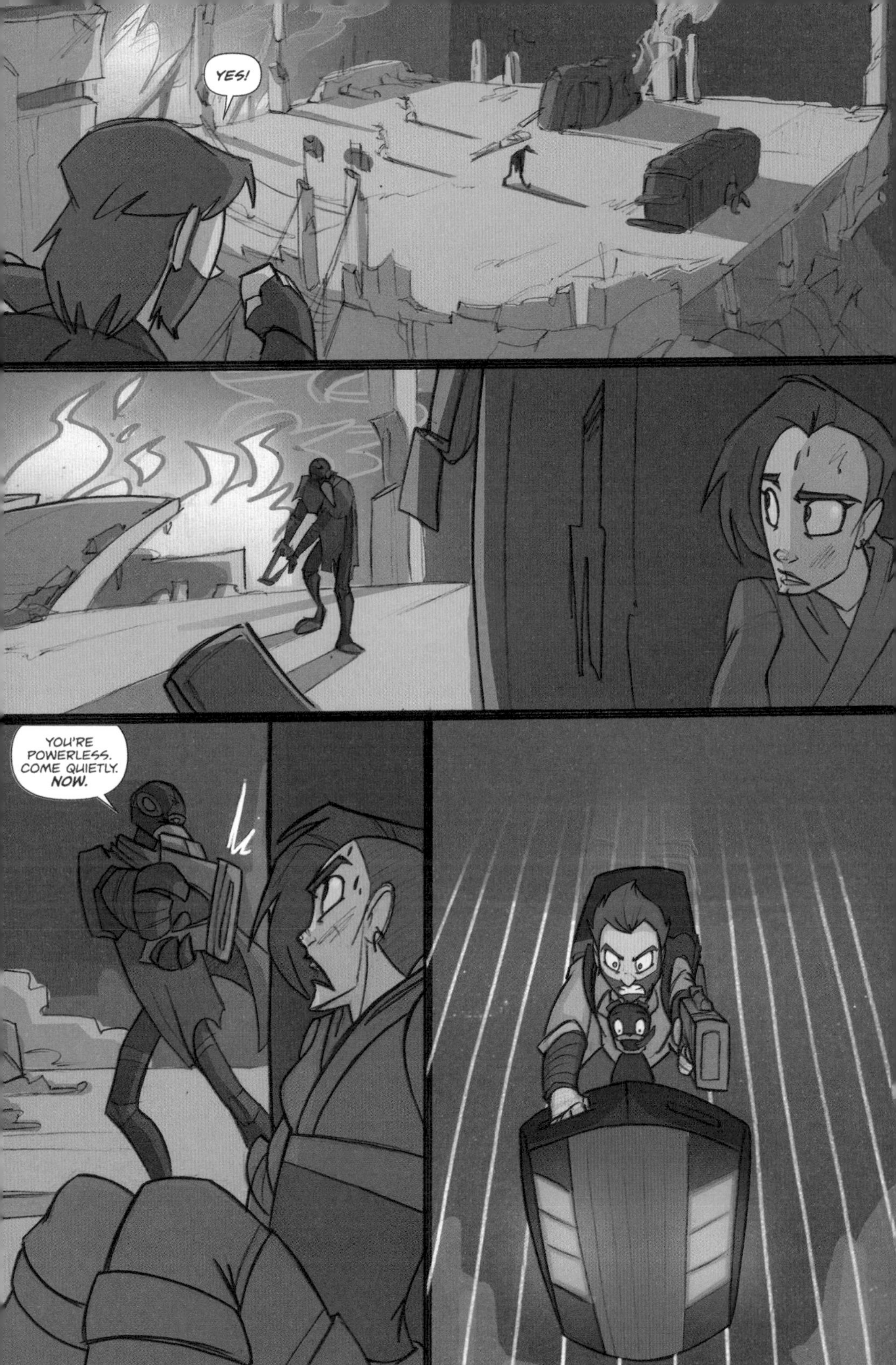
YES!
YOU'RE POWERLESS. COME QUIETLY. **NOW.**

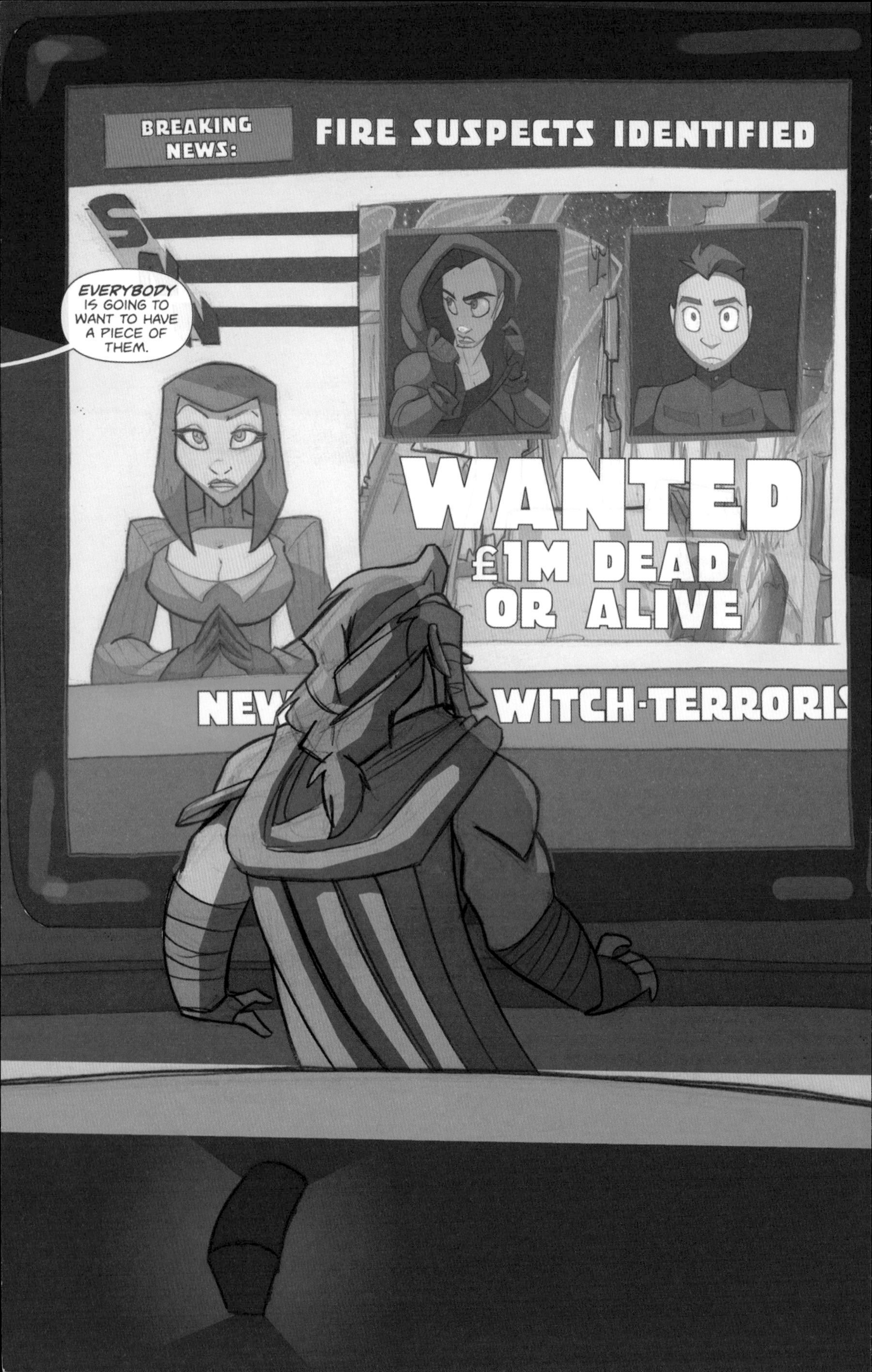
BREAKING NEWS:
FIRE SUSPECTS IDENTIFIED
EVERYBODY IS GOING TO WANT TO HAVE A PIECE OF THEM.
WANTED
£1M DEAD OR ALIVE
WITCH-TERRORIS

CHAPTER 3

THE ADVENTURE CONTINUES

Volume 2 | 48 Pages | £8.99

Buy online at www.BHPcomics.com | All good book shops

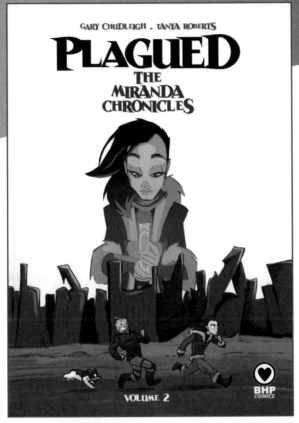

BHP COMICS

Check out more titles from BHP Comi

JACK LOTHIAN :: SHA NAZIR
LAPTOP GUY
FOREWORD BY JOHN WAGNER

GN / 84 pages / Full Colour / £7.99
ISBN: 978-1-910775-00-4

COMIC INVENTION

GN / 180 pages / Full Colour / £29.95
ISBN: 978-1-910775-03-5

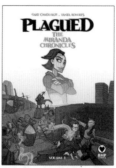

PLAGUED
THE MIRANDA CHRONICLES
VOLUME 1

GN / 64 pages / Full Colour / £8.99
ISBN: 978-1-910775-19-6

PLAGUED
THE MIRANDA CHRONICLES
VOLUME 2

GN / 48 pages / Full Colour / £8.99
ISBN: 978-1-910775-14-1

JACK LOTHIAN + GARRY MAC
TO MO RR OW

GN / 48 pages / Full Colour / £7.99
ISBN: 978-1-910775-05-9

FROM THE CREATOR OF JUDGE DREDD
ROK OF THE REDS
John WAGNER
Alan GRANT
Dan CORNWELL

GN / 144 pages / Full Colour / £18.99
ISBN: 978-1-910775-11-0

FRANK QUITELY
DRAWINGS + SKETCHES

GN / 128 pages / Full Colour / £18.99
ISBN: 978-1-910775-09-7
Hardback

Softback £9.99
ISBN: 978-1-910775-18-9

FULL COLOUR
A GRAPHIC ANTHOLOGY

GN / Black & White / £8.99
ISBN: 978-1-910775-15-8

WE SHALL FIGHT UNTIL WE WIN
A CENTURY OF PIONEERING POLITICAL WOMEN. THE GRAPHIC ANTHOLOGY.

GN / 64 pages / Full Colour / £9.99
ISBN: 978-1-910775-16-5

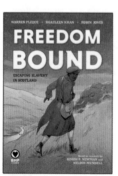

FREEDOM BOUND
ESCAPING SLAVERY IN SCOTLAND

GN / 144 pages / Full Colour / £19.99
ISBN: 978-1-910775-12-7
Hardback

Softback £14.99
ISBN: 978-1-910775-13-4

KILLTOPIA
キラー市

GN / 48 pages / Full Colour / £8.99
ISBN: 978-1-910775-17-2

The MIGHTY WOMEN of SCIENCE
"AN A-Z OF EXTRAORDINARY SCIENTISTS"

GN / 48 pages / Full Colour / £9.99
ISBN: 978-1-910775-06-6